Hiya!

I've loved the stories *Alice's Adventures in Wonderland* and *Through the Looking-Glass* for a very long time, so when I was asked to write a book with an Alice theme, I jumped at the chance. Alice has always been my fictional style icon – the original Tenniel illustrations of a girl with crimped hair, sticky-out skirts and hooped tights has always been my idea of cool, although as I get older I am toning down the look just a little! I also love the way Alice's story veers dangerously between dream and nightmare, and although I love the Disney movie and the more recent version with Johnny Depp as the Hatter, my fave film version is a moody black-and-white from 1966.

   I knew pretty much straight away that my take on the Alice story would be dark and a little surreal. I loved writing it, and I hope you will like reading it, too. Curl up with a hot chocolate and a jam tart, and let yourself fall down the rabbit hole too . . .

Cathy Cassidy, xxx

Cathy Cassidy

LOOKING GLASS GIRL

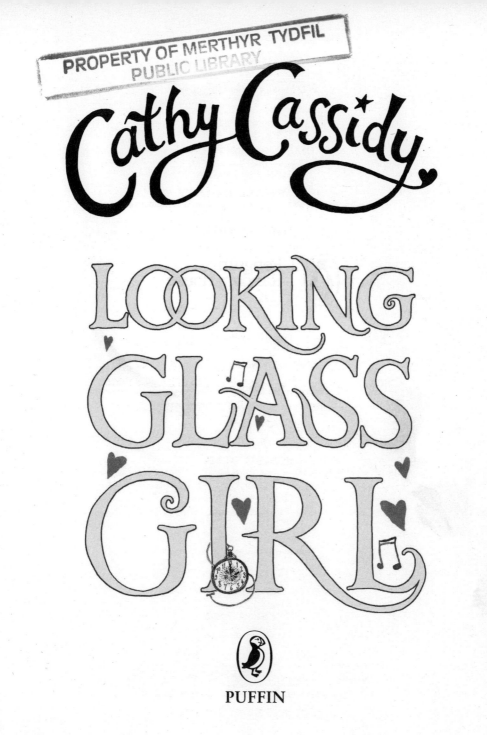

PUFFIN

PUFFIN BOOKS

UK | USA | Canada | Ireland | Australia
India | New Zealand | South Africa

Puffin Books is part of the Penguin Random House group of companies
whose addresses can be found at global.penguinrandomhouse.com.

Illustrations copyright © Erin Keen, 2015

The moral right of the author and illustrator has been asserted

Set in Baskerville MT Std 13.25/19.25 pt
Typeset by Palimpsest Book Production Limited, Falkirk, Stirlingshire
Printed in Great Britain by Clays Ltd, St Ives plc

A CIP catalogue record for this book is available from the British Library

HARDBACK
ISBN: 978-0-141-35782-9

TRADE PAPERBACK
ISBN: 978-0-141-35805-5

www.greenpenguin.co.uk

MIX
Paper from
responsible sources
FSC® C018179

Penguin Random House is committed to a
sustainable future for our business, our readers
and our planet. This book is made from Forest
Stewardship Council® certified paper.

1

'Emergency, which service?'

'We need an ambulance! Please, quickly!'

'I am transferring you now . . .'

'Hello, you are through to the ambulance service; how can I help you?'

'We need an ambulance, like, now! My friend has fallen and she's not moving and I think she might . . . look, we just need an ambulance, OK?'

'Where are you? Can you give me the address?'

'No! Oh, please, don't tell her, Yaz! I'm going to be in *so* much trouble!'

'We're all going to be in so much trouble. That doesn't matter right now; I have to tell her, Savvy – how else is the ambulance going to get here?'

I

'The address?'

'Hello? Sorry. We need an ambulance at 118 Laburnum Drive, Ardenley. You have to hurry! She's fallen and she's not moving . . .'

'She's not moving at all? Where did she fall from?'

'She fell down the stairs. It was an accident!'

'Have you moved her?'

'No, we're scared to – she's lying all funny. She's not moving at all. And there's all this broken glass and blood . . .'

'An ambulance is on its way to you now.'

'How long will it take? I'm so scared . . .'

'I need you to stay on the line. We'll be with you as soon as we possibly can.'

'It was an accident!'

'What is your friend's name?'

'Alice. Alice Beech . . .'

2

Alice

'Can you hear me, Alice? My name is Martin; I'm a paramedic. Hang on, Alice.'

Everything is dark; a thick, soft darkness that wraps around you like a blanket of sleep. I can hear someone talking to me, but I don't understand what he's saying – it's like some kind of secret code. It makes no sense at all.

'I'm calling in to report a head trauma victim, female, age thirteen; we're blue lighting her.'

Head trauma victim?

A shrill siren wail starts to screech, scratching its fingernails against my skin, filling up my senses. It makes everything hurt, but I can't seem to find the words to tell them to shut it up.

And suddenly I find myself falling backwards, down the rabbit hole, dropping like a stone. My screams are swallowed up by the soft blanket of darkness.

Year Six

I wasn't always a victim. Not so long ago, I was just a normal girl; a happy girl. I didn't get top grades in class and I wasn't the most popular kid in the school, but I had amazing friends and a happy family. I worried about all the usual things: test results, playground tiffs, whether I'd ever find a hobby I could be good at – something where I'd shine . . . but those worries never stopped me having fun.

And then, in Year Six, I was picked to play the lead role in our class production of *Alice in Wonderland*. I was so anxious that first night, I didn't think I could do it, but my best friend Elaine squeezed my hand and told me I'd be brilliant, and somehow I found the courage to step out on to the stage. It was only a school play in a draughty gym hall, but the audience whooped and whistled and stamped their feet, and I swished my sticky-out blue skirt and dropped into a curtsey, smiling so hard it made my face ache. I don't think I'd ever been so happy.

Elaine and Yazmina, my other best friend, only had small, non-speaking parts as two of the playing-card soldiers, but they were really pleased for me all the same.

'You were brilliant,' Yaz said. 'I could never have remembered all those lines!'

'And you got to do all those rehearsals with Luke Miller,' Elaine sighed. 'Lucky you! He's so cute!'

I laughed, but I wasn't crushing on Luke Miller like Elaine was. I'd known him since Reception class and I saw him as a friend – annoying sometimes but good fun as well. It had been fun working on the play with him, but Luke was going to Ardenley Academy after the holidays, so I knew I wouldn't see him again. Elaine, Yaz and I were all going to St Elizabeth's, a strict, all-girls school that was supposed to get great results.

I actually wished the whole lot of us were going to Ardenley Academy instead; we'd been to look at St Elizabeth's, and I'd hated the gloomy, dark panelled wood, the polished floors, the framed photographs of hockey and netball teams from years gone by that lined the corridor walls. I couldn't

5

imagine spending the next seven years of my life in a place like that, wearing a braid-trimmed blazer and a grey pleated skirt and knee length white socks. I mean, socks? Really? Not good. But Elaine and Yaz were both going there, so I buried my misgivings and signed up for it, and my parents were as proud as if I'd just passed half a dozen A levels with A* grades.

We finished Year Six on a high. Elaine, Yaz and I had mapped out our summer, planning sleepovers, picnics in the park, days out in town, backyard sunbathing sessions, but on the last day of term Miss Harper turned all that upside down. She handed me a flyer about a drama club that was running a summer school, and that changed everything.

'It's two days a week throughout the holidays,' she told me. 'A mix of kids, aged eleven to sixteen, all with a talent for acting. I thought that you and Luke would be perfect for it!'

I was so thrilled at being chosen, I didn't even notice the flickers of disapproval on the faces of my friends. I didn't notice anything until two weeks later, when I was at Elaine's house for a sleepover. I'd been talking about an improvisation exercise I'd done that day with Luke when Yaz interrupted me.

'Alice?' she said. 'No offence, but we're sick of hearing about your stupid drama club the whole time. And about Luke and what great mates you are these days. It's all you ever talk about, and it's getting boring.'

Elaine frowned. 'I know you don't mean it,' she said. 'But it's like you're rubbing our noses in it.'

I blinked. Had I been talking too much about drama club? About Luke? Did it sound like showing off? Maybe.

'Sorry,' I said. 'I suppose I do get carried away, sometimes. It's just that it's so much fun, and I know you'd absolutely love it, and . . .'

Yaz and Elaine exchanged an exasperated glance, and my words trailed away to nothing.

'It was just a fluke that they gave you that part,' Yaz said. 'I bet Miss Harper just thought of you because your name was Alice, and decided to give you a chance.'

'Anyone can act,' Elaine agreed. 'If we went to special lessons, we'd be good, too. But who wants all that stuff, anyway? Dressing up and playing games of "let's pretend".

I really didn't think Luke would go for that sort of thing. It's so babyish!'

After that, I was careful not to mention the drama summer school, or Luke. I kept my mouth closed and tried hard to be interested when they talked about boys and make-up and music, but it had knocked my confidence. Yaz and Elaine had never told me I was boring or babyish before; I'd thought they were happy I'd finally found something I was good at.

Instead of finding something cool to talk about when we were together, I became silent, anxious about saying the wrong thing. Yaz and Elaine had begun mentioning days out in town without me, a trip to the ice rink, a train ride to the seaside. I tried not to mind. I was going to drama club without them for two days a week, so I could hardly complain if they did things without me, but for the first time ever I'd begun to feel like they were deliberately leaving me out.

The summer turned sour. Sometimes, when I rang Yaz or Elaine, they didn't reply; if I tried their landlines, I'd be told they were out: at the cinema, or down at the park, or just 'out'. Often, they forgot to ring me back.

Maybe we'd been drifting apart, just a little, over the last year. Yaz and Elaine had sometimes rolled their eyes when I failed to summon up much interest in boy bands and crushes and turquoise nail varnish, but I hadn't thought those differences were fatal. I assumed we could find our way through them, like we always had before when one of us hadn't shared the others' passion for ballet or ponies or Harry Potter. I thought it would all blow over, but when Yaz had a sleepover the last weekend of the holidays and didn't invite me, it didn't feel that way.

We were supposed to start at St Elizabeth's together, the three of us against the world. Instead I pulled on my new uniform, complete with socks and braided blazer, and walked to school alone because they hadn't answered my texts. Without my friends, I was lost in a sea of uniformed strangers; adrift, lost.

I wanted to cry and yell and run away home, but you don't do those things when you're eleven. You tilt your chin and bite your lip and pretend you don't care.

St Elizabeth's did its best to keep groups of friends together, and I was put in the same form room as Yaz and

Elaine. My face lit up when I saw them that first day, and they smiled too, and for a moment I thought everything could still be OK for us.

'Hey, Alice,' Yaz said. 'How are you? We haven't seen you for weeks! How was your summer? How was that amazing drama summer school of yours?'

'It was great,' I said.

'I bet you made some cool new friends,' Elaine said.

I thought of how I'd got to know Luke better, how he was turning out to be a real friend and not just some boy from primary school; maybe even something more. I didn't think Yaz and Elaine would want to hear about that, though.

'Well, I've made a few friends,' I bluffed. 'They're all different ages, though, and I'm not sure any of them are at St Elizabeth's . . .'

'That's good, though,' Yaz told me. 'Meeting new people. Because we just haven't been on the same wavelength for a while now, have we?'

I bit my lip. 'Are you saying we're not friends any more?'

'Of course we're friends,' Elaine said. 'Obviously, we are! But that doesn't mean we have to be in each other's pockets all the time, does it? We should make new mates, see other people. We're growing up, moving in different directions. Maybe we just need some space?'

Space? I'd heard that line before, back when Elaine's mum left her dad. 'She just needs some space,' Elaine had said. 'They'll probably get back together. Maybe. Most marriages need that, just to stay healthy. Your parents should probably do it too; they might just be staying together for you and Nathan.'

'I don't think so,' I'd said, and Elaine's face had twisted up, making her look bitter and angry. I knew how sad she was feeling inside, so I didn't go on about Mum and Dad being happy; I didn't want to make her feel worse than she already did.

Elaine's parents never did get back together. Elaine's mum found herself someone new: a boyfriend called Kevin with no job and an attitude problem. He made Elaine's life a misery, and when Yaz and I went round for sleepovers he was so rude and grumpy Elaine had to stop asking us at all.

And now she wanted some space herself – from me.

'We're still friends,' Yaz clarified. 'But things are different

now, Alice. Let's enjoy secondary school. New starts, new challenges, new friends. Best of luck!'

They walked away and left me alone.

3

Alice's House

The house is a small, modern semi-detached at the end of a quiet cul-de-sac. The street lights throw a golden glow over the neat front garden with its clumps of bright daffodils and primulas, a child's BMX abandoned carelessly halfway up the path. Not even a curtain twitches as the police car draws to a halt outside. The houses are all in darkness, and a scattering of stars is visible in the blue-black canopy of sky above the street lights.

'Cold enough for frost tonight,' PC Lewis says, glancing upwards. 'Doesn't feel like spring at all . . .'

'Come on,' WPC James says. 'Let's get it over with.'

'I hate calls like this,' her partner replies. 'I have a thirteen-year-old daughter, too. Sleepovers. You think they're safe; you don't think things like this can happen.'

They walk up the path and ring the doorbell, leaning on it a little after the first few sharp rings. A light goes on upstairs, and a man's voice grumbles inside. 'All right, all right, take it easy, I'm on my way . . .'

A man in his late thirties wearing an outsize T-shirt and boxer shorts opens the door, and the officers watch as the colour drains from his face. They are used to this reaction; when two police officers arrive at your house in the middle of the night it is never good news.

'Mr Beech?' the woman police officer asks briskly. 'I am WPC James and this is PC Lewis. Can we step inside for a moment?'

'I'm Mark Beech. What's wrong? What's happened? Is it Alice?' The boxer-shorts guy is losing his calm, his voice rising rapidly into panic. 'Tell me!'

The police officers move past him into the hallway. A cat slinks past their legs, purring softly, and two more figures

14

appear on the stairs, a woman in a blue fleece dressing gown and a yawning boy of nine or ten in Batman-print pyjamas.

'What's going on?' the woman whimpers. 'Has something happened to Alice? What is it? Please say she's all right . . .'

'Your daughter Alice has been in an accident,' PC Lewis says, calm and reassuring. 'I'm afraid she has a head injury. She has been taken to Accident and Emergency at Ardenley General Hospital.'

'Oh God!' the woman cries. 'A head injury? An accident? How? She was supposed to be at a sleepover! I don't understand!'

'As far as I know, the accident took place at 118 Laburnum Drive,' WPC James explains. 'It appears that Alice lost her footing, fell down some stairs and struck her head against the tiled flooring of the hallway.'

Mark Beech pulls on a jacket, grabs his car keys from the hall table and then stalls abruptly, as if suddenly aware that he is barefoot and wearing boxer shorts.

'I don't understand,' Laura Beech is saying. 'How could

that happen? At this time of night? Where were Savannah's parents? Why didn't they call us right away?'

'I believe Mr and Mrs Hunter are away for the weekend,' WPC James says. 'An older sister was left in charge, but it's not clear whether she was on the premises at the time of the accident. We have informed family services . . .'

'But Alice is OK?' Laura Beech presses. 'It's not serious?'

'As I explained, she has a head injury,' PC Lewis states, unable to meet her gaze. 'The doctors are in the best position to explain what's going on.'

'This can't be happening,' Laura Beech says. 'I want to see her – I have to see her now!'

'We can take you to the hospital, if you'd like?' PC Lewis offers. 'Or you can drive yourself, if you feel OK to do that.'

'I'll drive,' Mark Beech says. 'Nathan, mate, go and put on something warm, and I'll just–'

He shrugs helplessly and runs up the stairs in search of shoes and trousers.

The two police officers drive away from the house. Less than two minutes later, the Beech family is out of the house and in their own car, huddled and uneasy, driving through the night.

'Is Alice going to die?' Nathan asks into the silence, and Laura Beech begins to cry.

4

Alice

'Alice, my name is Dr Fleet. Can you hear me? You've been in the wars, I'm afraid. You've had a fall and taken quite a knock to the head, and I think you've hurt your arm as well. We're going to do some preliminary tests and assessments; see how best we can help. I'd like you to open your eyes now if you can hear me, Alice. Just for a moment; open your eyes . . .'

'Alice?' the voice says, and someone shakes me gently by the shoulders. 'Wake up! Wake up! We're late!'

I sneak a glance through half-closed eyes and gasp in horror at what I see; white fur, a twitching nose, long ears that droop and graze softly against my cheek. A white rabbit in a waistcoat and jacket is leaning over me, huffing and sighing and rolling its eyes.

The White Rabbit. From Alice in Wonderland.

I am not joking.

'Alice? Come on!' it says, sounding annoyed. 'We're late!'

I know it's a dream, of course. I'm not scared.

I sit up straight and open my eyes . . .

Year Seven

I thought that perhaps Elaine and Yaz were punishing me, making a point with this whole 'giving me space' thing. They were annoyed that I'd been busy in the holidays, maybe a little jealous that I'd been picked for the drama club summer school, that I'd been able to get to know Luke better, but I was sure they'd get over it. I thought that at any moment they might look across and pull those stupid, comic faces we used to make when we were little, say, 'Ha! Fooled you!' and we could all be proper friends again, instead of being in this horrible semi-detached limbo where they'd throw me the occasional smile and ask how my day had been, and then walk away and leave me. That didn't happen.

Elaine and Yaz got friendly with two girls called Savannah Hunter and Erin Stewart who sat near them. Erin was clever and confident, and Savannah was one of those girls everybody wants to know; she was tall and pretty with waist length caramel-coloured hair and golden-brown skin. She had the kind of easy confidence that made the St Elizabeth's uniform look like high fashion on her, and she was always laughing.

'She used to go to my old dance class,' a quiet girl called Serena said to me in the changing rooms one day after PE. 'Savannah. Her parents are really rich and her mum takes her to a beauty salon every month to get a spray tan and her nails and eyebrows done. Pathetic, huh? She's just fake, fake, fake.'

I wasn't sure about that. I thought that maybe Serena was jealous, because she had thick glasses and unplucked eyebrows and nails that were bitten down to the quick. Her skin wasn't golden-brown but the kind of white that looks bluish in the winter, mottled pink with the start of teenage acne.

I was pretty sure that Savannah would look just as good without the spray tan and the pencilled-in eyebrows. It

20

was something to do with the way she laughed; the way she shook out her hair like she didn't have a care in the world.

'She's a bully,' Serena whispered. 'She has a mean streak. If you're not in her group, watch out!'

Savannah didn't look like a bully, but I was worried all the same. What if she reeled in Elaine and Yaz and then ditched them? I didn't want that to happen, but maybe, if it did, they'd realize what true friendship was and come back to me. I still thought things could work out, even then.

I looked at the advice pages of my favourite teen magazine for ideas for reviving a flagging friendship; it recommended talking things through, suggesting exciting new things to do together, reminiscing about the happy times we'd shared.

So I tried. I waited until Savannah and Erin weren't around and one morning in late September I walked right up to Elaine and Yaz, smiling my brightest smile and trying to pretend I wasn't terrified they'd laugh in my face.

'Hey,' I said. 'I noticed there's a youth club starting down at the community centre – every Thursday evening, seven till nine thirty. Music, dance, sport, crafts . . . it sounds OK. We always said there should be one. D'you fancy it?'

Elaine and Yaz had often grumbled that our town needed a place for teenagers to get together; a place to listen to music, hang out, meet boys. I thought this would appeal to them, but they just looked at me, blank and disapproving, like I'd suggested we take up macramé or stamp collecting.

'Youth club?' Yaz said. 'I don't think so, Alice. That's so lame. It's for losers. Well, yeah, actually, you might like it – but we already have a social life, thanks very much.'

I reeled from the words as if I'd been slapped.

Elaine shrugged and smiled as if she didn't quite approve of what Yaz was saying, and later on I saw her alone by the lockers. I screwed up every last bit of courage I possessed and walked over.

'Elaine?' I asked. 'I thought we were friends. Just what exactly did I do to make you and Yaz hate me so much?'

She had the grace to blush. 'We don't actually hate you, Alice,' she said, as if explaining something complicated to a small and particularly stupid child. 'Don't be silly! We've just grown apart, yeah? It happens. It's nothing personal.'

It felt personal to me. These were the girls I'd known since Reception class, the girls I'd shared my hopes, dreams and fears with. We'd shivered together in a badly-pitched tent on Brownie camp-outs, whispering secrets late into the night. I'd held Yaz's hand, back when her gran died, wiped her tears, stood next to her at the funeral in a black dress and shiny shoes. I'd listened over and over to Elaine's troubles round about the time that her parents were divorcing, then listened all over again when her mum moved in with the horrible boyfriend.

I knew that Yaz loved Harry Styles and peanut butter KitKat Chunky bars and that she had wanted a dog ever since she was tiny, but knew it would never happen because her dad was allergic to pet fur. I knew that Elaine wanted to be a top model and live in Paris and wear scarlet shoes with bows on the ankles and six-inch heels, and that she wanted to marry Luke Miller, or at least go out with him.

She sometimes got huffy and moody if she didn't get what she wanted, but nobody was perfect, right?

Yaz and Elaine knew me, too; they knew that I still slept with a lamp on even now, because I was scared of the dark, that I was afraid of ghosts and couldn't watch horror films because they gave me nightmares. They knew that I dreamed of going to drama school, of being an actress one day.

'We used to have some great times,' I reminded Elaine. 'Rehearsing for the play; me as Alice and you as playing-card soldiers . . .'

Elaine just rolled her eyes and shrugged.

'So are we friends?' I pressed. 'Are we just taking some time out, like you said? Giving ourselves some space?'

'It's not working out,' she said, biting her lip. 'Savvy doesn't like us hanging out with losers. Not that I think you're a loser or anything! It's just . . . well, like I said. Nothing personal.'

'Savvy doesn't like it?' I echoed, and Elaine looked guilty, embarrassed.

Savannah had reeled them in all right, and what she said was law. Our friendship was over, finally, with no hope of reprieve. I hated Savannah then. I hated her so much it was like an ache inside me.

24

Tears stung my eyes.

'You can always hang out with your new friends from drama club,' Elaine suggested awkwardly. 'You don't need us.'

'Well, thanks,' I said bitterly. 'It was nice knowing you. I think.'

I went back to the teen magazine for more advice; it said that if all else failed, the best plan was to let go and move on. Well, let's just say that advice failed too.

The following week, Nick from the drama club told us that they'd had their funding cut by the council and would be closing. My new friends vanished overnight, scattered across the town in their different schools.

'Keep in touch, Alice, OK?' Luke Miller said, scribbling his landline number on a scrap of paper because he didn't have a mobile. I kept that scrap of paper in my pocket for a year, until it disintegrated, but I never did call him. I didn't have the nerve.

At St Elizabeth's, even Serena got fed up with hanging out with me and attached herself to a group of science club kids.

I had nothing to do but watch my old friends sparkle and

shine. Savvy and Erin were pretty and popular and cool, and very soon Yaz and Elaine were, too.

Me? I was the geek, the loner.

I was nobody at all.

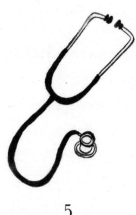

5

Ardenley General Hospital

Accident and Emergency is not a good place to be in the early hours of a spring Sunday morning. The Beech family have to dodge a drunk singing 'Bohemian Rhapsody' in the middle of the waiting room, and wait at the desk while a young man with a black eye and a cut lip yells at the receptionist before storming away into the night. A nurse with a clipboard ushers them along a grey corridor lit by flickering fluorescent strip lights.

They walk past a row of curtained cubicles. Some of the curtains are open, and Mark Beech glimpses a small boy hunched over on a trolley, crying; an elderly woman having her blood pressure taken; a worried mother pacing the floor with a screaming toddler.

The nurse leads them into a small waiting room with soft chairs and gossip magazines spread out across a coffee table, gesturing for them to sit. 'Dr Fleet will be with you shortly,' she says kindly. 'He can explain how Alice is doing.'

'Where is she?' Laura Beech pleads. 'I need to see her! Now! Please?'

'All in good time,' the nurse says kindly. 'Help yourself to tea or coffee.'

The door clicks softly behind her as she leaves.

Alice's little brother slumps on to a chair and begins to kick absently at the coffee table. For a minute there is no sound except for the thump-thump of his trainers against the underside of the table, getting gradually louder and more forceful.

'For God's sake, Nathan!' Mark Beech yells abruptly. 'What are you doing? Your sister is seriously ill! Show some respect!'

Nathan stops kicking, his lower lip quivering. A moment later Dr Fleet walks into the silence, and everyone turns to look at him.

'How is she?' Mark Beech demands, his voice still gruff from the telling off. 'Alice? What happened? Why can't we see her?'

'You can see her,' the young man promises. 'You can see her very soon. I am Dr Fleet; I'm one of the team who've been helping to treat and stabilize Alice. She has had a serious fall; she has a broken arm and a nasty cut to the side of her face; it seems a mirror fell on her on the way down . . .'

'Oh, Alice,' Laura Beech whispers.

'Our biggest concern right now is the head injury Alice sustained when her head struck the tiled floor. She has not yet regained consciousness, which is not unusual after such a fall, but it does indicate the need to give her a CT scan to find out what's happening. The scan will show us if there are any fractures to the skull, or any internal bleeding.'

'You're saying she may need surgery?' Mark Beech asks.

'Let's see what the CT scan shows,' Dr Fleet says. 'We'll know what we're dealing with then.'

Dr Fleet leads the family into one of the curtained cubicles they passed just minutes ago, and there is Alice, lying on a wheeled bed, pale and motionless. A crescent-shaped cut starred with criss-cross Steri-Strips curves from temple to cheekbone, and her right arm is strapped and folded into some kind of sling. There's a tube in her mouth which seems to be regulating her breathing; various other wires and tubes attach her to a series of machines.

'Oh,' Laura Beech reaches out a trembling hand to touch her daughter's cheek, then stops short. 'Oh, Alice . . .'

6

Alice

'Alice? Can you hear me, Alice? It's Mum! I know you're sleeping now, but I just wanted to let you know I'm here. We're all here, me and Dad and Nate. The scan is nothing to be scared of, I promise you. Alice? Can you hear me?'

'Can you hear me, Alice?' the White Rabbit asks. 'Can you hear me?'

Before I can answer, the noise begins. It fills the air, a cacophony of drumming that blots out everything else. I fall to my knees and cover my ears with my hands, but the uproar is inside my head, beating against my skull, threatening to break it apart.

I close my eyes and wait for the pain to stop.

Year Eight

I watched them change before my very eyes, Elaine and Yaz. Actually, I should say Lainey and Yaz, because Elaine ditched her name for something much cooler just a few weeks into secondary school.

Lainey and Yaz were like caterpillars who suddenly morphed into beautiful butterflies without having to endure the ugly chrysalis stage. They just woke up one morning and spread their wings and that was that; they were away, fluttering high above everyone else's heads; dazzling, daring, out of reach.

Yaz started wearing eyeliner and straightened her hair every morning. Lainey dyed her hair from mouse brown to blonde at half-term and pretended the sun had bleached it on her holiday to the Canaries.

They looked great, but when their sparkling smiles accidentally swept across me, they froze like ice. My ex-best friends were cold, careless, detached. It was like I'd never known them at all.

Mum knew that things had gone wrong with Yaz and Lainey; she'd have had to have been blind not to notice.

The girls I'd spent every spare minute with right through primary had dropped out of my life like they'd never been there at all.

'Are you settling in OK?' Mum had wanted to know. 'Making new friends?'

'Sure,' I lied. 'It's a great school. Everyone's really nice!'

'Well, if you ever want to invite anyone over for tea or for a sleepover, go ahead,' Mum said, and I'd smiled and said I would, but of course it didn't happen. Who would I have asked?

Mum didn't mention it again. I think she knew how much I was struggling, but she didn't want to make me feel any worse than I already did.

The bullying started in Year Eight.

It began slowly. It was subtle, clever, the kind of thing you probably wouldn't even notice if you weren't the target. My shoe went missing from the changing rooms after a PE lesson and turned up in a flower bed outside. The following week, my school tie vanished and I was given a detention. Random stuff kept turning up in my school bag, too. We had assembly two or three times a week, and had to leave our bags at the back of the hall, so I knew the sabotage was happening then. Once it was a can of Coke with the ring pull removed so that it leaked and made dark, sticky stains all over everything; once a smooshed up fish paste sandwich which wrecked all my books and made everything stink; once it was an actual raw egg.

There were a dozen small things: a glass of water spilled over my dinner at lunchtime, a test tube full of sulphur knocked out of my hands in science, the word 'loser' scrawled on my bag in Sharpie pen, a half-chewed toffee stuck in my hair after I'd been foolish enough to sit in front of Lainey and Yaz in English.

I remembered what Serena had once said about Savvy being a bully, but it was always Lainey and Yaz who did her dirty work. Savvy kept her hands clean, and even dished out a compliment or two.

'Wow, Alice, your hair really suits you like that,' she said, the day after I changed my parting to disguise the place where I'd had to chop the mess of toffee out of my hair. And, 'Oh, is that a new bag? How cute!' the day I came into school with my little brother Nate's Power Rangers rucksack after the Sharpie pen incident.

Savvy always looked wide-eyed and innocent when she

said these things, and it kind of messed with my head, but then I've never been quick on the uptake when it came to sarcasm. I knew Savvy was behind the bullying, pulling the strings. Hadn't Lainey told me last year that Savannah didn't like losers?

Once, in art, I made a little clay coil pot that was pretty much perfect and earned some praise from the teacher. Savvy, sitting across the table from me, glanced at my creation and then back at her own misshapen pot.

'That's brilliant, Alice,' she announced, sounding slightly amazed. 'The best one in the class. You're really good at art!'

It should have been a warning. As we were clearing away at the end, Lainey somehow nudged the pot with her elbow so that it fell on the floor, flattened and spoiled. 'Oh no!' she exclaimed. 'I'm so sorry, Alice! I'm so clumsy. It was amazing, too!' She bent to rescue it, squidging the clay together in her fist so there was no hope of patching it up. 'Never mind; you can just start from scratch next week.'

Nobody else had even noticed, or perhaps it was just that nobody else cared.

A flash of anger made me tug Lainey's sleeve as she turned away from me to throw what was left of my pot into the scrap clay bin.

'Why are you doing these things?' I whispered. 'You and Yaz? Can't you just leave me alone?'

Lainey bit her lip.

'I'm sorry,' she said, and for a moment I thought I could see the old Lainey there, behind the dyed blonde hair and the swagger. It gave me hope. 'It's just, well, Savvy doesn't like you.'

I took a sharp breath in.

'So do you do everything Savvy tells you to?' I challenged her, and Lainey just shrugged and looked sheepish. I saw her then for what she was: weak, cowardly, easily led. It made me feel sad.

I looked across the room to where Savvy was pulling on her blazer, picking up her teal-blue leather satchel, flicking back her hair. As I watched, she caught my eye and smiled and waved.

I hated Savvy Hunter more than anyone else alive, but I had to admit she had style.

7

Cafeteria, Ardenley General Hospital

It is one thing to huddle in the family waiting room at Accident and Emergency wearing mismatched nightwear, another entirely to be sitting in the hospital cafeteria at midday, wearing faded pyjamas with a grey coat thrown over the top, your hair still fluffy, tangled and uncombed. Laura Beech knows she looks a wreck, but she doesn't care. She cradles a mug of tea that went stone cold half an hour ago and stares into the distance, wondering how exactly this can be happening to her.

Mark has taken Nate home to wash and dress; Mark's mum will meet them at the house and look after Nate for the day.

Laura's head is a whirl of fear. Two hours ago, Dr Fleet had explained that Alice's CT scan showed a small area of internal bleeding.

'We will operate to stop the bleed and relieve any pressure,' he explained. 'Alice's condition is critical, but this operation will give her the best chance of a healthy recovery.'

Critical. What did that even mean?

Mark had signed a consent form, his hand shaking.

A nurse encouraged them to take Nate home and pass him into the care of his grandmother, but Laura would not leave the hospital. 'Have you eaten?' the nurse asked. 'Had a drink, even? You need to stay strong, for Alice.'

Laura cannot imagine being able to eat, but the idea of tea sounded vaguely possible.

'The operation will take time,' the nurse had said. 'There is nothing you can do until it's over. Go and sit in the cafeteria for a while. Eat something. Dr Fleet is the best there is, and I will fetch you if there's anything to report at all.'

'Do you promise?'

'I promise.'

Laura watches the clock on the wall, which seems to have

been stuck at the same time for about a hundred years. Perhaps it is actually broken?

Upstairs somewhere, a surgeon is cutting into her daughter's skull and lifting away a sliver of bone, poking a scalpel blade into the soft, dark space beneath.

Laura's hands shake so hard she drops her mug of tea, splattering the table and the floor with rivers of pale brown liquid.

8

Alice

'Alice, this is Dr Fleet. In a moment we'll be taking you down to theatre. You've hurt your head and we have to stop the bleeding, and once we've done that, all being well, you will be on the mend again. I'll be working alongside our consultant neurosurgeon, Mr Williams, and he has been doing this job for twenty-two years, so I promise you he knows what he is doing. I am confident that between us we can get you well again, Alice. We have a great team looking after you today. You're in good hands.'

Good hands. A white furred paw presses down on my arm, insistent.
Do paws count as hands?

'She's asleep again,' a puzzled voice says. 'Really, that girl is always sleeping!'

'Has she hurt herself?' a second voice wonders. 'She's very pale.'

'Shhh, just let her rest.'

I can feel soft paws stroking hair back from my forehead, and just as I'm beginning to relax, something cold and sharp scrapes against my temple and a piercing pain shoots through my head.

Good hands, bad hands, safe hands, dangerous ones – how can you tell?

I remember other hands, jabbing and poking and pushing at me in the dark. And everything is darkness now, heavy and stifling, weighing me down like a blanket made of stone.

January

I didn't tell anyone about the bullying.

I didn't tell the teachers because I was pretty sure they wouldn't believe me. Savvy had them all eating out of the palm of her hand; she was clever as well as pretty – she got good grades and earned extra good-girl kudos by being on the student council and running the local half-marathon to raise money for Children in Need. The teachers thought she was golden.

I didn't tell Mum because I didn't want her to feel sorry for me – well, sorrier than she already did. She knew I didn't hang out with Lainey and Yaz any more and she must have guessed there was nobody at school I was close to because I never talked about anyone, never brought friends home.

'I didn't meet my best friends until I got to university,' Mum told me once. 'Not everybody finds the right people at school, you know. Whoever said that school days are the best days of your life was talking a lot of rubbish, Alice.'

I pretended not to know what she was talking about.

I didn't tell any of my classmates either, because I didn't think they'd care.

I became invisible. On rainy lunchtimes I lurked in the school library; on sunny days I sat outside on the wall by the gym and read a book or ploughed through some homework, hoping that nobody would notice me.

I was an outcast, a loser, a waste of space. I kept my eyes

down so I couldn't see my ex-best friends sneering at me, so I couldn't see Savvy waving and smiling her fake, fickle, shiny bright smile.

I woke up every morning with a dull ache of dread inside me. I hated school. I had no clue how I was going to endure another five years of it.

And then one day my drama teacher asked me to stay behind after class. She told me the school was putting on a production of the Shakespeare play *A Midsummer Night's Dream*. It was mainly the Year 11, 12 and 13 students, but there were some openings for younger pupils too.

Drama was the only class I really loved, the only time in school I actually felt happy. It was partly to do with the fact that Savvy, Erin, Yaz and Lainey weren't in the same class, but mostly because drama gave me the chance to escape my life. In drama, I didn't have to be me any more.

Miss Copeland said I had talent, potential. She wanted me to get involved in the school play.

Just like that, I had something to wake up for, something to work for, something to be a part of. I was given the part of Cobweb, a servant of the Fairy Queen, and though it wasn't a big part, it changed everything.

Finally, I had somewhere to go at lunchtime; somewhere I was useful, wanted, worthwhile. I didn't have many lines to learn, but extra people were always needed to help paint scenery, make props or adapt costumes. People spoke to me, and I replied, and although I was rusty by then at knowing what to talk about, it was fun to talk about books and plays and acting techniques, exams and eyeliner and how weird it was for some of the girls who were dressing up as male characters in tights and boots and velvet hats with extravagant feathers.

Those rehearsals were a little window of normality and friendliness in my day. They made the rest bearable.

One day, I bumped into Keisha Carroll beside the lockers at breaktime. Keisha was a Year 13 girl with a lead role in the play – she was a brilliant actress, and she was also beautiful, cool and kind. She was friends with everybody, even the Year Eight nobody with a tiny role, the girl who painted scenery and helped with the props; me. Keisha was buzzing that day. She'd just heard she'd been offered a place at uni to study drama after the summer. She showed me the letter and I told her I was happy for her, and she gave me a little hug and said she was buying chocolate to share out at the rehearsal later, to celebrate.

I was grinning as I watched her walk away, because I was genuinely pleased for her, and also because I couldn't remember the last time someone had treated me as a friend, an equal, outside of the rehearsal rooms at least. As for the hug, it was like a small miracle. I hadn't had a hug from a friend since primary school.

As I turned away from the lockers, Savvy Hunter appeared at my side.

'I didn't know you knew Keisha Carroll,' she gushed, giving me a wide-eyed, smiley look that almost fooled me into trusting her.

'We're in the play together,' I said. *'A Midsummer Night's Dream.'*

Savvy raised an eyebrow. 'Wow, that's so cool! We should get together, Alice, talk about it sometime.'

I was pretty sure she was joking, but I was willing to play along. 'Sure we should,' I said.

Savvy smiled. 'Well. I'm having a sleepover the weekend

after next. You should come. Yeah, that would be cool! I'll send you an invite.'

I didn't believe for a minute that she meant it, of course. But it turned out that she did . . .

9

Intensive Care Unit, Ardenley General Hospital

By Sunday night, Alice is hooked up to an oxygen tank and an intravenous drip. A spaghetti dinner of wires and tubes and lines connect her to a jumble of monitors that purr and bleep and pulse. Her head is bandaged; her arm set in a plaster cast.

The family watch from behind a wide glass window as inside the room a nurse checks the machines, changes the IV drip and makes notes on a clipboard.

'Everything went as well as we could have hoped,' Dr Fleet is telling them. 'The bleed has been stopped, there are no areas of pressure and of course the broken arm has been set; we have done everything we can for now. The rest is up to Alice.'

'When will she come round?' Laura Beech asks. 'How long until the anaesthetic wears off?'

'The anaesthetic should be out of her system soon,' Dr Fleet says. 'But as for when she might regain consciousness, it's impossible to say. In other circumstances, Alice would have woken up by now, but as you know, that hasn't happened. With a head injury like this, coma is not uncommon. It can last for a few minutes or hours, or it can last – well, very much longer than that.'

Mark Beech looks up, his face bleached of colour.

'Are you saying that she could be unconscious for days?' he demands. 'Or weeks? Months? Years?'

Dr Fleet sighs. 'I'm saying that we have no way of knowing.'

'But, I don't understand,' Laura says. 'The operation was a success; you've said so, doctor. So surely she'll be fine?'

'The human brain is a complex organ,' the doctor explains. 'There is a great deal we have yet to learn about it. In cases of head injury and trauma, the mind can shut down for a short time, even though there may be no obvious physical cause. We don't yet fully understand why this happens; perhaps it is a way of dealing with the pain, or allowing all the body's resources to focus on healing.'

'Like sleep,' Laura says, softly. 'She's sleeping . . .'

'There are significant differences,' Dr Fleet says. 'At the moment, Alice is not responding well to external stimulus. Her breathing has been steady, and we are hoping to detach the ventilator shortly, but in every other respect her body is functioning at its lowest level. The coma may last for a few hours, a few days, or much longer, just as you have said. At this stage, we don't know, but from a physical viewpoint there is no reason to believe Alice is not capable of making a full recovery. There is no longer any physical cause for the coma, so we are hoping she will regain consciousness in due course.'

'Can she hear us?' Laura asks. 'Does she know we're here?'

'I can't tell you that for certain,' Dr Fleet replies. 'Some coma patients can hear and understand what is going on around them, so by all means talk to Alice. Speak to her as if she were listening. For all we know, she may be.'

The doctor moves on to see another patient, another family, and Mark and Laura Beech go back into the ICU room to be with Alice. The lights have been dimmed and in the half-light, if you took away the ventilator, the drips, the constant flashing and bleeping of the monitors, you might imagine that Alice was just sleeping. She looks so peaceful, Laura thinks.

You would never guess that she's drifting, lost in another world.

10

Alice

'Alice, it's Mum. The doctors say there is no reason why you should not make a good recovery, but head injuries can be complex and there are lots of things we don't yet fully understand. Well, I don't fully understand any of it. I can't see how you would come to fall down a flight of stairs at one o'clock in the morning, all by yourself. If I could turn the clock back I would never have let you go to that sleepover. I'd have kept you close where I could look after you. I love you, Alice. Please come back to us soon . . .'

'Alice!' a voice roars. 'Alice! Come back here at once!'

A firm hand tugs at my shoulder and I turn around to see the

Duchess, grim-faced, a squalling baby wrapped in a blanket held firmly against her shoulder.

'I must get ready for the Queen's croquet match,' she says. 'Here. I want you to look after this.'

She shoves the squirming baby at me, and I hold it at arm's length, unimpressed. It is a very ugly baby, with big flapping ears and a squashed red nose. I look more closely: I am holding a small, grunting pig. As I watch, the pig squirms and jumps right out of my arms, trotting off towards the woods, its curly tail waving, and I begin to follow.

'Alice, come back!' the Duchess bellows behind me. 'Come back here right now!'

March

The Monday after Savvy Hunter had told me she might invite me to her sleepover, I was sitting alone in the corner of the school canteen as usual, picking at the remains of a veggie lasagne and killing time before rehearsals. A shadow fell across the table, and Savvy slid into the seat beside me, lining up her tray alongside mine.

Erin, Lainey and Yaz followed, filling the empty seats around me. Savvy, as always, radiated a shiny, smiley aura of happiness. The others were less enthusiastic, flicking uneasy glances at me and picking listlessly at their plates of salad. It was awkward.

'So, I was thinking,' Savvy began. 'We've never got to know one another properly, have we, Alice? And I'd really like to, because I actually think you're pretty cool.'

My first impulse was to laugh; big mistake.

As if to destroy Savvy's misconceptions before she went any further, I ended up half-choking on a spoonful of fruit salad; Savvy patted me on the back and said something kind about how the canteen fruit salad couldn't really count as salad because it seemed to be all apple and orange with never anything exciting like strawberry or kiwi. I just coughed and went a dark shade of crimson.

'So yeah, I'm really interested in all your drama stuff and everything,' Savvy ploughed on. 'You're just, like, soooo talented! Lainey and Yaz have been telling me how you had the lead part in the school play back at primary . . .'

I could just imagine.

'Anyway, like I said, I'm having a sleepover this weekend,' Savvy went on. 'To celebrate the start of the Easter holidays and stuff. I'd love it if you could come – I've made you an invite, and everything!'

She took out an envelope with a photocopied image of Alice in Wonderland stuck to the front, pushing it across the table towards me.

'It's an Alice-themed sleepover,' she explained, looking round at the girls. 'We like to do cool, quirky stuff like that, don't we? And I thought that if we were asking you, an Alice theme would be just perfect! We can have a Mad Hatter's tea party and dress up and stuff . . .'

I looked across at Lainey, Yaz and Erin, who seemed uneasy, unimpressed.

'You can be Alice, obviously,' Savvy declared. 'I mean, you probably have a costume and everything, don't you? Or you could get something from the drama group. I just think it would be awesome, don't you?'

I couldn't work out if Savvy honestly thought the idea

of an Alice-themed sleepover was cool, or if it was some kind of elaborate joke designed to make fun of me. I noticed that Lainey was shaking her head slightly as if she really didn't approve of what was going on.

That was my clue, surely. The girl who'd been getting her minions to bully me for the last year was raising the stakes, stepping things up a level. Savvy was a game player; she wanted to lure me right in, laugh at me, humiliate me. Did she really think I'd be stupid enough to fall for it?

I opened the envelope and looked at the homemade card inside, cut into the shape of a teacup. I tried to imagine Savvy decorating it with collaged *Alice in Wonderland* images, writing out the date, time, address and dress code in her cool, curly handwriting. It was a lot of trouble to go to, to make someone feel bad.

And an *Alice in Wonderland* theme – well, maybe that was a sign that I should take a risk and go? I couldn't be sure.

'Please come,' Savvy was saying, and she turned that doe-eyed gaze on me again, the one that made me forget that behind the shiny, smiley mask she was a cold-hearted bully. 'I think we'd really get on. I think we could be friends!'

I opened my mouth to say no, I really did.

'That would be awesome,' I said.

11

The Copper Kettle Cafe, Ardenley, Monday

Savannah, Erin, Lainey and Yaz are sitting at a window table, cradling mugs of hot chocolate, their faces shadowed and anxious.

'She had to have brain surgery,' Yaz says, stirring her hot chocolate listlessly. 'That's really serious, right? My dad and her dad work together, and apparently Mr Beech said it was a life or death situation.'

'I heard she was in a coma,' Lainey chips in. 'My mum met her gran at the shops this morning. Apparently Alice has been unconscious ever since the accident. She might lose her memory. Or have brain damage or something. So yeah, that's pretty serious, I'd say.'

Erin frowns. 'What if . . . what if she . . . well, doesn't pull through?'

'Shut up!' Savvy snaps, slamming her mug down on the table. 'She won't die! She can't! Don't even say that!'

The girls are silent, eyeing Savvy warily. She doesn't lose her cool often, but today she is visibly shaken. The shiny, smiley mask has slipped; her eyeliner and mascara have smudged, giving her panda eyes, but nobody dares mention it.

'Oh God,' Savvy wails. 'I am in *so* much trouble. Mum and Dad are furious. I am grounded for a month, except that they can't actually enforce it because they're at work and it's the Easter holidays. But still, it's bad. And they are raging at Carina, which means she is raging at me. It's all so, so unfair!'

'It's a nightmare,' Yaz agrees.

'You were only trying to be nice,' Lainey tells Savvy. 'You just wanted to include Alice; you weren't to know what would happen.'

'*I* wasn't to know?' Savvy echoes. 'Lainey, there were four of us involved. Don't try to lay all the blame at my door! You were the one who took it too far. I told you that was out of order! Don't kid yourself – we're all in this together.'

Lainey shifts, uncomfortable. 'Well, obviously,' she says. 'And I know I got things a little bit wrong, but I didn't mean Alice any harm. Nobody did! All I meant was . . . well, it *was* your idea.'

'I knew it!' Savvy howls. 'You do blame me! Carina blames me, my parents blame me. I bet Alice's parents blame me, too. The thing is, Lainey, yes, it was my idea to invite Alice over. Yes, it was my idea for us to dress up. Yes, it was even my idea to liven things up a bit, but not everything was my idea, OK? Not everything!'

Erin puts a hand on Savvy's arm. 'Nobody's saying it was your fault,' she says softly. 'It was an accident! Just a stupid accident! Nobody was to blame!'

The four girls look at each other, then away again. Lainey starts chewing her nails, Erin fiddles with her iPhone, Yaz drops a sugar lump into her hot chocolate and stirs it noisily.

Savvy's eyes brim with tears and she wipes them away savagely with the back of a hand, adding to the panda effect.

'If nobody was to blame, how come we lied to the police?'
she asks.

Nobody can even begin to answer that.

12

Alice

'Alice, it's me, Nate. Mum says you're sleeping because you hurt your head and you need time to heal. She says that you can hear me, and if you can I think you should probably wake up now, because everything has been rubbish since you hurt your head. Dad is moody all the time and Mum keeps crying, and I have to stay at Gran's and she won't let me play on my Xbox. So I'm just saying, wake up, Alice, because it's a rubbish Easter holiday without you.'

I have hardly stepped into the trees when I see the Lory, bedraggled and forlorn, perched on a rock.

'It's all your fault,' the Lory says. 'You've ruined everything!'

'What have I done?' I ask, and the Lory sighs and shudders, ruffling its dripping feathers.

'Why, you fell, of course!' it says. 'You fell into this dream, and now nothing is quite what it used to be!'

'I don't think it can have been my fault,' I argue. 'I think you're wrong! I should know, after all!'

'Not at all,' the Lory says, sulkily. 'I am older than you and should know better.'

When I asked the Lory how old it was, it just stared at me with disgust. 'Don't you know?*' it asked. 'Don't you know anything?'*

And I realized that I didn't. Not anything at all . . .

March

I told myself that I could always change my mind about the sleepover. I didn't have to go; didn't have to risk being laughed at, picked on, ridiculed. I could just say no. Deep down, though, I knew I was going to go; a tiny part of me wanted to believe that Savvy really did like me.

If I could do the right things, say the right things, perhaps Savvy, Erin, Lainey and Yaz would see that I wasn't a bad person, a sad person or a loser. I wouldn't have to sit on my own in class, hide in the library at breaktime, paint scenery in the drama block at lunchtime. Perhaps I could change things, if I really, really tried.

What did I have to lose?

I found a blue dress in the costume cupboard in the drama block and borrowed a net petticoat so I could make it stick out. I still had the little white apron and the hooped tights from when I played Alice in Year Six.

'Whose sleepover did you say it was?' Mum wanted to know. 'Savannah's?'

'She's really nice,' I said. 'It'll be fun . . .'

I didn't know if either of those things were true.

'It's nice to see you making new friends,' Mum said. 'I know it hasn't been easy for you –'

'I'm fine, Mum,' I lied. 'I've told you. I have plenty of friends at school.'

Mum sighed. 'I know, I'm sure. It's just that I've always felt Elaine and Yaz treated you badly. Of course, friends

63

do drift apart sometimes, but those girls were terribly jealous of you.'

'Mum,' I interrupted. 'Elaine and Yaz will be at the sleepover too. They're friends with Savvy.'

Mum's forehead creased with anxiety. 'I see. So, this sleepover, Alice. Is it about trying to patch things up with Elaine and Yaz?'

I knew Mum was worried, and I knew she had good reason to be, but the questions bugged me. Mum had no idea how hard things were for me at school; how badly I needed a friend.

She didn't know how it felt to be alone, watching your ex-best friends have fun without you. She didn't know what it was like to stay in the shadows, wishing you had the courage to step into the light. Yes, I wanted Yaz and Lainey back. Was that so wrong?

I didn't care that they'd treated me like dirt; I was willing to forgive. I could picture a scene where we all said sorry, where past hurts were packed away and never spoken of again. Maybe Savvy would be the peacemaker, realizing at last that I wasn't just a victim but a potential friend? But

even if that didn't happen, I had got to the point where I didn't think I'd care if I was the bottom of the pile in Savvy's little gang – I just wanted to be on the inside, not the outside.

It sounds pretty desperate, put like that, but I was exactly that; pretty desperate.

'I don't think I'd be happy about you being friends with Yaz and Elaine again,' Mum said, gently. 'Once people know they can get away with treating you like a doormat, they tend to keep on doing it. Be careful.'

'I'll be careful, Mum,' I said, annoyed. 'Whatever.'

'I'm just worried, Alice,' she said. 'I'm thinking of you.'

'Look, it's not about getting Yaz and Lainey back,' I lied. 'They'll be there, but that's no big deal. It's Savvy and Erin I want to be friends with.'

Mum nodded and smiled, but I'm not sure she believed me.

'I like Savvy,' I said in the end, and it was true, because even though I knew she was a spoilt, selfish diva, I couldn't help but be charmed. Call me shallow, but I wanted to be a part of her world.

I loved the idea of a sleepover where you dressed up; it seemed creative, cool and quirky. It seemed like Wonderland to a girl like me.

13

Carrow Park, Ardenley

Lainey is sitting on a park bench; she is balancing on the backrest with her feet on the seat, drinking a Coke and huddling into her jacket. Yaz is lying back on the bench, staring up at the starless sky. The March days are cold and crisp and bright, but the nights are down-right arctic.

Yaz thinks that if she has to stay on this bench for much longer she might just freeze to death and be found there in the morning, frozen solid, her hair and eyelashes dusted with icing sugar frost.

'Savvy's losing it,' Lainey says, taking a swig of Coke and handing the can down to Yaz. 'She's cracking up. If we're not careful, she'll blab something to her parents and then we'll all be in trouble. Or, worse, she'll try to blame it all on me; she's thinking that way, I know she is!'

'No way,' Yaz says, reassuring. 'Maybe you lost your temper with Alice a little bit, but . . .'

'Seriously, Yaz, you too?' Lainey growls. 'Look, OK, I was upset with her, but I didn't want her to fall. It wasn't my fault!'

'Of course it wasn't!' Yaz agrees. 'I know that, and Savvy knows that. We all do. If anything, Savvy feels responsible. The sleepover was at her house, and it was her idea to invite Alice.'

'Great idea that turned out to be,' Lainey says.

'Savvy wasn't to know what would happen,' Yaz points out. 'Nobody could have known.'

Lainey drains the last of the Coke and scrunches the can up before throwing it through the air; it misses the bin and clatters away into the darkness.

'Let's be honest,' Lainey says. 'What we did to Alice was mean. Some people might say it was bullying. I might have said some things I shouldn't have . . .'

Yaz stands up abruptly, tugging down the sleeves of her coat, fishing in her pocket for chewing gum. 'It's pointless going over all that,' she says. 'You were upset. We'll stick together and nobody needs to know exactly what happened . . .'

'Unless Savvy blabs,' the other girl scowls.

'She won't,' Yaz says. 'It was an accident, like I said. Maybe we haven't always been as nice as we could have been to Alice, but she never seemed to get the message, did she? Always looking at us with those sad eyes, moping around by herself, trying to make us feel guilty. The thing is, not all friendships are forever. Alice couldn't seem to see that.'

'She sort of asked for it,' Lainey admits. 'Hanging around us, trying to find things to chat about, like the last two years just didn't even happen . . .'

'Why did we fall out?' Yaz asks, frowning. 'I can't even remember. It was something to do with her being in the play, right? It was all she could talk about for a while. And then she got picked for that summer drama school . . .'

Lainey jumps down from the bench and the two girls begin walking towards the park gates, heading for the bus stop.

'Alice was a pain,' Lainey says. 'Back then, anyway. She always had to be the centre of attention. She thought she was better than us.'

'Maybe we were just jealous,' Yaz suggests. 'I know I was pretty insecure back then. I remember feeling hurt that Alice got picked for the play, and then picked again for the summer school. I felt like she was rubbing my face in it.'

'I wasn't jealous,' Lainey says. 'I just never understood what people saw in Alice Beech. She was so . . . mousey. Dull. I think we just grew out of being friends. We moved on, she didn't. It happens.'

The girls arrive at the bus stop and huddle together in a pool of light from the street lamp, waiting.

'It's a mess,' Lainey says. 'I wish Savvy hadn't asked her to the sleepover.'

Yaz sighs. 'Me too. It wasn't our best idea. We used her, and it backfired on us big time. It was just supposed to be a bit of fun. Alice totally overreacted. If she hadn't got so upset, the accident would never have happened.'

70

'It wasn't our fault,' Lainey repeats, as if saying this often enough will make it true. 'We just have to keep our cool, stick to our stories. And Savvy needs to chill and get a grip.'

14

Alice

'Alice, this is Gran. I've come to sit with you for a little while because your mum's popped home to have a sleep and a shower. I know you're sleeping, chick, and that's great, but we are all so worried about you so please don't sleep too long. When I go home I'm going to do some baking, Alice. Jam tarts. D'you remember when we used to make them together, when you were very little? I'd make the pastry and you'd roll it out and cut the circles. And you'd spoon in the jam, just the right amount – and eat a few sneaky spoonfuls straight from the jar, when you thought I wasn't looking. Yes, I'll make jam tarts and bring them in tomorrow . . .'

A dishevelled figure is running wildly towards me out of the trees; the White Queen, her arms stretched wide as if she were flying, her hair falling down and her shawl trailing behind her. She comes to a halt in front of me, bewildered.

'Everything is coming undone,' she says. 'That's the effect of living backwards, you see. It can be very confusing!'

'Living backwards?' I question, wrapping the shawl around her and fixing her tangled hair back into place. 'I never heard of such a thing!'

'There's one advantage,' she tells me. 'Your memory works both ways.'

'I'm not sure my memory works at all,' I confess.

'Of course it does,' the Queen declares. 'Do you recall having jam yesterday?'

'No,' I admit.

'Well, what about jam tomorrow?'

'That's nonsense,' I protest. 'How can I remember something that hasn't happened yet?'

The White Queen shakes her head. 'You're going to have to, Alice,' she says. 'You're going to have to remember everything, if you want to get out of here . . .'

Last Friday

At the last moment, I almost lost my nerve.

All week I had studied Savvy, like she was an especially challenging subject I needed to learn inside out for an exam. She was amazing. She looked flawless – like her skin had been airbrushed, her eyeliner painted on so perfectly that not even the strictest teacher thought to tell her to wipe it off. Her caramel-coloured hair was glossy and thick, like something from a shampoo advert, and she was the only girl at St Elizabeth's who could make knee-high socks and a pleated skirt look cool.

She broke the rules, but only in small ways. A French manicure, the faintest whiff of vanilla perfume, lace-up black boots with a little Louis heel; Savvy was such a perfect pupil that she got away with it all. She always came top in French – rumour had it her uncle had a house in Provence which they visited every summer – and she was effortlessly good at English, geography and music. She played the piano at grade four level and regularly represented the school at athletics; she'd won a silver cup last September for the high jump, and medals for the javelin and relay.

So yeah, she was a model pupil. Everyone wanted to be like Savvy Hunter, except for Serena with her sour stories of long-ago bullying and game-playing. Then again, nobody actually listened to Serena, even if we suspected her words might be true.

People wanted to think the best of Savvy – even I did, and I knew better than most how cruel she could be. That was her magic – a way of seeming to be bright and beautiful and kind, in spite of it all. We wanted to believe in her.

The more I studied Savvy, the more panicky I got. Maybe it was exam nerves – I knew a whole lot about my subject, but I was certain I'd forget it all on Saturday night. I could have sat a multiple-choice exam paper or written a three page essay on Savvy Hunter, but hanging out with her was a different story. I was bound to mess up.

What did they even want me there for? Savvy didn't need new friends. She had three best friends already, and most of our year thought she was the coolest thing since strawberry cream frappés; any one of them would have loved an invitation to her house. Why would she pick me, of all the girls at St Elizabeth's, to come to her sleepover?

It had to be a prank, a joke, a trap. At best I'd be an outsider; at worst, a victim, just waiting to be baited, tormented.

Paranoia seeped into my blood like poison.

Savvy Hunter looked like butter wouldn't melt in her mouth, but I knew the truth, even if I tried hard to ignore it.

I swallowed back an ocean of regret and shame and accepted that I wouldn't be going to Savvy's on Saturday night. I must have been crazy to think I could.

But how to tell Savvy? All week she'd been reminding me of the sleepover; a wink in French, a wave in maths, a winning smile on the netball courts in PE. Today she'd stopped by my table in the school canteen and asked if I was all set for Saturday; if I had my costume sorted, if I was looking forward to it.

'Can't wait!' I'd said, in spite of my misgivings.

Yeah, right. I was a coward as well as everything else. Maybe I'd just text Savvy at the last minute with an excuse; I'd say I was too sick, too sad, staying in to wash my hair. I cringed at the thought. If going to Savvy's sleepover scared me, not going scared me more. Overnight, I could see my status dropping from mere loser to spineless, saddo, pondlife scum.

Walking home from school on Friday, I saw Lainey leaning against the bus stop, alone, chewing gum and tapping out messages on her smartphone. I took a deep breath and walked right up to her.

'Hey,' she said, her face bored, impassive. 'All sorted for tomorrow?'

'About that,' I said. 'I've changed my mind. I think we both know it's not a good idea.'

Lainey's face changed, registering annoyance, alarm. 'You have to come!' she argued. 'Savvy's put loads of work in to make it cool for you. She'll be gutted if you don't turn up! She's really interested in getting to know you – she wants us all to be friends!'

I raised an eyebrow. 'Really?' I asked. 'Why? A fortnight ago, she barely knew I was alive. I was just some loser to pick on, play tricks on.'

Lainey looked uncomfortable. 'I'm sorry about that,' she said. 'Savvy did think you were a bit of a loser back in Year Seven – she said you were clumsy, clueless. She encouraged Yaz and me to pull a few pranks. I suppose we wanted to

impress her, and we thought it was funny to make you look bad. I'm not sure why we thought that now, but . . . well, we did.'

It felt like Lainey had pushed me on to the pavement and kicked me in the ribs with her pointy school shoes. The pain was sharp, shocking; it took my breath away. Lainey and Yaz, my ex-best friends, bullied me because they thought it was funny?

Lainey touched my arm. 'Look, Alice,' she said softly. 'We were stupid. Wrong. We were out of order, Yaz and I, and we want to put it right. We've been telling Savvy what a cool person you are; how we used to be really good friends. We suggested she might ask you along to one of her sleepovers.'

'You suggested?'

'Well, yeah. And Savvy was fine with it. I mean, I'm not saying she's going to want to be your new best friend; she doesn't accept just anyone into her friendship group. She plays games with people sometimes, but she doesn't mean any real harm.'

I blinked hard, because I really, really didn't want to cry in front of Lainey. I wasn't sure whether to be hurt about how she had treated me, or happy that she wanted to put it right. As for Savvy being a game-player, that was nothing I didn't already know. She was the puppet master and Lainey and Yaz were her puppets; I knew all too well who was pulling the strings.

'I have feelings, Lainey,' I said, as calmly as I could. 'I'm not some toy for you and Yaz and Savvy to pick up and put down when you feel like it. I'm a person, not a game!'

'I know that!' Lainey argued. 'I swear I do. I'm not proud of how I treated you, Alice. Call it insecurity, hormones, jealousy; call it what you like, but I know I was wrong. I want to fix things, I really do. That's what this sleepover is about – for me, anyway. Please come. I won't let Savvy do anything mean. No games, no pranks. OK?'

Right up until a day or so ago, I'd have turned my back on all the bad stuff I'd been through in a heartbeat just to have my old friends back. Now, I wasn't sure.

The hurt of what Lainey had said was lodged in my heart like a rusty blade.

Lainey sighed. 'It's no excuse, but the last few years have been pretty awful for me, you know. Family stuff. I think I was kind of jealous of you; your family were lovely, and mine . . . well, things were the opposite of lovely, as you know. It was just like everything started to go right for you at the same time as it was going wrong for me, and it didn't seem fair. It was childish and stupid of me to think that way, and I want to put that right. Please come tomorrow, Alice. For me? I'll stick up for you, I promise.'

I wasn't sure if I could trust Lainey's promises, not any more, but I wanted to. I wanted to more than anything else in the world.

15

Alice's House

It is half past two on Tuesday afternoon and Laura Beech is fresh out of the shower and asleep on the sofa, a duvet pulled over her head to block out the daylight. She is sleeping on the sofa because it is right next to the phone, and she doesn't want to miss a call from the hospital with news. She didn't want to leave the hospital at all – not while Alice was still unconscious, but even the doctors and nurses have been telling her she needs to get some proper sleep.

Laura is pretty sure sleep isn't an option, but the moment her head hits the pillow she is gone, lost in a series of dark

dreams that morph seamlessly into nightmares of falling, falling, falling.

A siren shrills, jolting her awake, and it takes a moment for her to realize that the phone is ringing. She snatches it up, still groggy from sleep.

'Mmmph . . . hello? Has something happened? Is something wrong?'

'No, no, nothing's wrong,' an unfamiliar voice says. 'At least, nothing else. Am I speaking to Mrs Beech?'

Laura shrugs off the duvet and struggles into an upright position. 'Yes; who's calling?'

'This is Jenny Hunter, Savannah's mother. I'm just calling to offer you my support, and to see if there's been any change in Alice's condition. As you can imagine, Savannah has been worried sick . . .'

Laura feels a surge of anger flood through her; Jenny Hunter, Savannah's mother, the woman who went away for the weekend and left a houseful of teenagers to fend for themselves.

'No change,' she says through gritted teeth. 'Alice is still in a coma. We're lucky she's alive!'

There's a brief pause at the other end of the line, then

the voice is back, smooth and placatory. 'I can't tell you how sorry we all are. Such a dreadful, dreadful accident. It's shaken us all up terribly. I believe Savannah was trying to befriend Alice, because she was very quiet at school, but of course, it all went terribly wrong . . .'

'You could say that,' Laura grates out. Inside, she is boiling with anger; she wants to shout and scream and throw the phone across the room. She wants someone to blame, and this Jenny woman is an easy target.

'If there's anything at all we can do . . .'

Laura tries to bite her tongue and fails. 'It's a little late for that,' she says. 'Perhaps if you'd been at home on the night of the accident, looking after those five girls instead of flitting off to enjoy your luxury break in . . . in . . . Cornwall, was it? Perhaps that might have helped. Because I can't help feeling that something very strange was going on when everyone but Alice was fast asleep in bed at one in the morning, and yet she was fully dressed and wearing a coat and shoes as if she was planning to come home.'

'My elder daughter, Carina, was keeping an eye on them,' Jenny protests.

♡ ♥ ♠ ♡ ♦ ♣ ♡ ♥ ♠ ♡ ♦ ♣ ♡

'Not very well, by all accounts,' Laura snaps, but her anger is ebbing away now and tears threaten. 'Not very well!'

'Oh, Mrs Beech, all this must be dreadful for you,' the voice sweeps on. 'And of course I feel terrible that we weren't there, but that weekend had been planned for months; it was our wedding anniversary. And then at the last moment Savannah said she wanted a friend to come over – Erin. I didn't want to disappoint her. And of course Carina is seventeen and very responsible; and she promised she'd look after everything. I had no reason to believe that anything could or would go wrong!'

Laura can feel herself folding, crumpling and curling up in a sad, defeated slump.

'Savvy didn't mention anything about Yaz and Lainey and Alice, but of course I know now that she'd invited them over too,' Jenny Hunter says. 'I have had a very stern talk to Savvy about that; about honesty and respect. If it's any consolation, she is very sorry. We all are. Nobody had any idea things could turn out like this!'

'No. No, of course not,' Laura concedes. 'I'm just – well, worried sick. And very, very tired.'

Jenny Hunter bulldozes on, but her voice is kinder now. 'You poor, poor woman – I can't begin to imagine how you're feeling. I know in your shoes I'd be going out of my mind with worry. Is there anything I can do? Drop off a casserole? Help with lifts? Get some groceries delivered? I have an account with Ocado; it would be no trouble at all. Just let me know.'

'No, no; we're fine,' Laura says, her voice no more than a whisper.

'Well, that's all I was ringing for, really. To pass on my condolences. Oh, that's probably not the right word – my sympathy. You know what I mean. Savannah really is very distressed; she's been asking me if she can visit, but I don't suppose . . .'

Laura thinks of Alice, lying in the wheeled bed with the white coverlet in the Intensive Care Unit, the tangle of wires and the jumble of monitors bleeping and pulsing, the nurses gliding soundlessly in to change a drip, check on blood pressure, administer meds. She doesn't want anyone

to see her daughter like that; a shell of a person, broken, lost.

Then again, perhaps Jenny Hunter and her daughter should see just what they've done.

'I'll ask about visitors,' she says. 'I'll ask.'

16

Alice

'Hello there, I'm Mr Williams, the neurosurgeon who operated on you a few days ago. How are you? I hear you're doing very well, very well indeed; I'm hoping that you'll be back with us shortly. Now, I'm just going to go through the reactive tests again, so if you can feel anything, please let me know.'

The Caterpillar looks at me for a few moments in silence. 'Well,' it says at last, languidly. 'Who are you?'

I open my mouth to answer, and then falter. It feels like a trick question.

'I knew who I was when I got up this morning,' I say, uncertainly. 'But I've changed a few times since then . . .'

'What do you mean by that?' the Caterpillar demands. 'Explain yourself!'

'I can't,' I argue. 'Because I'm not myself! I can't remember things as I used to.'

'Remember what things?' the Caterpillar asks.

My mind reaches out for a wisp of memory; but there's nothing there at all.

Saturday

I put on the blue dress, arranged the net petticoat underneath so the skirt flared out, vintage style, then tied on the white apron. I used crimpers to sizzle my mouse-brown hair into tiny, perfect waves and tied in a thin blue ribbon.

I looked in the mirror and saw a girl I barely recognized. She looked different from the Alice who'd played this part almost two years ago; she was older, wiser, warier. Life had not worked out the way she'd imagined, and I could see a sadness in her eyes and wished it wasn't there.

I twirled in front of the mirror and my dress swished

pleasingly. The sticky-out skirt made my waist look tiny and the fitted top showed off curves that definitely hadn't been there two years ago. The stripy tights gave the whole thing a kind of cool, anime twist and I was wearing black Mary-Jane shoes with a little heel; I'd customized them by sticking on red felt hearts and ribbon bows. I'd spent an hour trying to get my eyeliner just right, testing out different versions of barely-there smudgy eye shadow. I'd borrowed Mum's mascara but didn't dare try it for fear of poking myself in the eye and ending up looking bloodshot and pathetic.

I smiled as brightly as I could, chasing away the sadness. Tonight, just maybe, I could peel away the last eighteen months, start over. Dressed as Alice, I felt stronger – more like my eleven-year-old self, the girl who had owned the makeshift stage at George Street Primary and wowed the audience into a standing ovation. OK, not all by myself, maybe, but I had definitely been a part of it.

I had loved that feeling; there was nothing else like it in the world. I'd felt brave, beautiful, invincible – and maybe I could feel that way again.

I remembered, just after the play, reading the sequel to

Alice in Wonderland; it was called *Through the Looking-Glass*. In that book, Alice didn't fall down a rabbit hole; she pushed through the mirror above her sitting room mantelpiece and got back to Wonderland that way.

I pressed a palm against the cold, shiny mirror glass now, but it didn't give way. I guess that would have been way too easy, but I couldn't help wishing I could step through the glass into a world where everything was subtly different; a world where I had friends.

Instead, I had no option but to do it the hard way.

A sleepover at Savvy's house. It was like being offered a plate of cakes, each one with an 'eat me' label attached, and having to choose. I had no way of knowing if the cake I picked would make me taller or smaller, brighter or cooler or maybe just freakishly weird. If only I could stay calm, hit lucky and pick the right one.

I wasn't kidding myself; there would only be one right choice, and it was more than possible that I'd mess up and end up worse off than ever.

Still, I figured it was worth the risk.

Right now, I had nothing to lose. So what if the whole night turned out to be a nightmare? So what if Savvy

♡ ♥ ♠ ♡ ♦ ♣ ♡ ♥ ♠ ♡ ♦ ♣ ♡

planned to have a laugh at my expense; if Lainey failed to stop her? It didn't matter, because it would be no worse, no different from what I was already living with. I'd survive.

And if I managed to say the right things, do the right things, make the right impression? Well, my life would change forever. I didn't trust Savvy Hunter and a part of me was scared of her, but still, I knew that she was my way out of obscurity. I was kind of in awe of her.

I gave a little wave to the girl in the mirror, and she waved back, smiling, as if she knew something I didn't.

I pulled on a duffel coat because the weather was still cold for March, and picked up my holdall, carefully packed with pyjamas, sleeping bag and a Tupperware box of jam tarts I'd made that morning with cute pastry hearts on top. Gran had showed me how to make them when I was really little, and they were the one thing I knew I could get right. I didn't know if Savvy would think they were cool or child-ish; I'd just have to hope for the best.

'Have fun, sweetie,' Mum said as I came downstairs. 'Remember, if there's any problem, or you want to come home early . . .'

'I'll be fine,' I insisted. 'Don't fuss.'

'Well. You know where we are. Do you have your mobile?'

'Yes, Mum.'

Dad was giving me a lift to Savvy's. He didn't talk much as we drove across town; just told me it was nice to see me going out again, seeing friends.

'This Savvy lives on the posh side of town, doesn't she?' he remarked as we turned off the main road and drove towards Laburnum Avenue. 'Big houses.'

Dad was right; the streets here were wide and tree-lined, the houses tall red-brick Victorian semis with fancy bay windows. It didn't surprise me – I'd heard the rumours at school about her living in a posh house. And Savvy had looks and charm and popularity, so why not money too?

I asked Dad to stop on the corner so that I could walk the last little way to number 118 and he didn't frown or argue like Mum might have done. Perhaps he knew I needed that last couple of minutes alone to gather my thoughts and my courage.

I had left Alice Beech behind. I walked along the street, my heels clicking against the pavement, my crimped hair lifting a little in the breeze, candyfloss light. With every step I felt stronger, braver; a fizz of excitement ran through me.

What was the worst that could happen? That they hadn't dressed up, that it was all a prank designed to make me look silly? I could handle that. I thought I could handle most things. I wanted to make Savvy glad she'd invited me. I wanted to have fun, and if that wasn't possible, I would pretend, act my way through.

Looking over my shoulder, I saw Dad indicate and turn the car, driving away with a little toot of the horn. I half raised my hand to wave, then opened the gate of number 118 and walked along the path, passing rows of graceful red tulips. The front door was painted a glossy royal blue and had a stained glass window and an old-fashioned letter-box made of shiny brass.

I pressed the doorbell, took a deep breath and prepared myself to fall down the rabbit hole.

17

Ardenley General Hospital, Wednesday

Mrs Hunter is half hidden behind the biggest bouquet of flowers imaginable. Her daughter Savvy is carrying grapes, chocolate, a teen magazine; she looks scared – a million miles from the cool, confident girl who rules Year Eight at St Elizabeth's. Her eyeliner is perfect, her glittery eyeshadow unsmudged, but still, her eyes look pink from crying.

'Goodness,' Laura Beech says. 'What amazing flowers! Are they for Alice?'

'We thought she might like them,' Mrs Hunter says. 'Brighten the place up!'

'Well, yes,' Laura agrees, taking the flowers and looking

around for a nurse. Flowers are not allowed in Alice's ICU room – it is all monitors and screens and smooth, scrubbable surfaces – but a helpful ward assistant takes the flowers, finds a vase and makes a nice display in the visitors' waiting area.

'I brought these,' Savvy says, holding out her own offerings. 'So she doesn't get bored. And you always bring grapes to people in hospital, don't you?'

'I'm sure she'll love them, when she wakes up,' Laura agrees.

'She's still unconscious?' Savvy checks. 'Does that mean . . . well, will she be all right, when she wakes up? Will she be, you know, normal?'

Laura feels the breath catch in her throat. This is a question she hasn't dared to ask, hasn't even dared to think. But the doctors would have mentioned it, surely, if they felt that Alice might wake up somehow damaged. Not normal. The question tries to lodge itself in Laura's mind, but she brushes it away impatiently and smiles brightly.

'Yes, she'll be fine, absolutely fine, don't worry.'

Savvy nods, reassured. 'And will she lose her memory?

I've seen things on TV where people in a coma wake up and can't remember anything. Do you think that might happen?'

Mrs Hunter frowns. 'Savannah, that's enough; we're here to visit and be supportive, not to interrogate!'

Laura lets her gaze drift away to the window of Alice's room. Inside, her daughter lies still and silent; a girl frozen in time. Laura knows the questions are natural, inevitable, and she tries to answer truthfully.

'We don't know yet, Savannah,' she says. 'Right now we're so focused on waiting for her to wake up that we haven't thought very far beyond that. There's no reason to suppose Alice will have memory loss, or any other problems, but it's certainly possible. It was kind of you to come, Savannah; we're hoping that having one of her friends talk to her could help to bring Alice back to us.'

'So she'll be able to hear me?' Savvy asks. 'I can talk to her?'

'I'm pretty sure she'll be able to hear you,' Laura says. 'You can just chat away as normal; that's what I do. The doctors say it might help. Shall we go in?'

She ushers Savvy into the room and gestures towards the chair at the bedside. Savvy perches on the edge of it, looking terrified.

'Alice?' Laura says, stroking her daughter's pale cheek. 'Your friend is here – Savannah. She's been so worried about you, but hopefully now she can see that you're definitely on the mend. I'll leave you two girls together, shall I?'

Savvy watches Alice's mum retreat, hears her asking Mrs Hunter if she'd like a coffee. The two of them move out of earshot, out of sight, and Savvy leans forward, her lower lip trembling, and forces herself to look at Alice.

'Can you hear me, Alice?' she asks. 'Can you, or are they just pretending, just kidding themselves? Because you don't look like you're asleep, Alice. You look really sick, and all those wire things . . . those machines . . . it's scary. I hope you get better. I hope you do wake up, because I have seen on TV and in the papers about people who stay in a coma for years and years, and never, ever wake up. I couldn't stand it if that happened to you, Alice.'

Savvy reaches a hand out across the white waffle coverlet, letting her fingers touch Alice's.

She bites her lip. 'I just . . . wanted to say I'm sorry.'

18

Alice

'I hope you can hear me, Alice. It's Savvy, OK? I hope you wake up soon and that you're all normal and stuff; I really do. I just sort of hope you can't remember everything that happened at the sleepover, and if you can . . . if you do . . . well, please don't tell them. Please?'

I'm lost. The trees close around me, shady and dark, and a mist slides around me as I walk. The mist seems to be inside my head as well as outside it, and it scares me. And then, out of the mist, comes a Fawn, a small deer that looks as frightened as I feel.

'Hey, hey,' I say, holding out my hand. 'Can you help me? I think I'm lost!'

'We're all lost, here,' the Fawn says. 'In these woods, nobody can remember anything . . . and nobody knows who to trust. Beware!'

'I can trust you, though, can't I?' I ask, and the Fawn just looks at me with huge, helpless eyes. I put my arms around its neck and we walk on together until the mist thins and the Fawn breaks free, disappearing into the trees again.

Can I trust her? I wish I could remember.

Sleepover

Savvy answered the door dressed as the White Rabbit, complete with waistcoat and pocket watch and fluffy white ears. She was wearing white tights, a little white skater skirt and white Converse. The tip of her nose was painted black, and long, spidery whiskers had been painted on her cheeks. She looked cute and quirky and beautiful in a way I knew I never could.

'Alice!' she said, her face lighting up at the sight of me. 'You're here! Come in, come in!'

She led me inside, smiling, complimenting my dress, my shoes, my hair. 'Oh, Alice, you look amazing,' she said. 'Wow, you are so creative; I just knew you'd love the fancy-dress theme! Wait till Lainey, Yaz and Erin see you! We're just through in the lounge.'

I followed Savvy through the hallway, and it did feel a little bit like Wonderland. The place was amazing. The hall floor was all Victorian mosaic tiles and there was a vase of red and white roses on a curved hall table at the foot of the stairs. I caught sight of myself in a huge antique mirror that rested on the table: a fleeting glimpse of long hair, smiling face, blue dress. It felt surreal.

Savvy led me into the lounge – which was pretty much the size of our entire house – and there were the others, draped across the fancy L-shaped sofa, face-painting noses and whiskers on each other and taking pictures of their new Alice-themed selves. There was an actual chandelier glittering above our heads and a big, abstract painting on the wall that looked like something my little brother might have done in playgroup, way back when. It was probably worth thousands.

Lainey was dressed as the Cheshire Cat. She looked nothing like the fluffy ginger version in the book and the films, though – her take on Cheshire involved black tights, black leotard, black velvet ears and a swishy tail that swayed as she moved. Erin was the Dormouse, in a beige onesie, and Yaz was the March Hare in brown leggings and a drapey brown tunic top and crêpe paper ears that kept falling down over one eye.

'Look at you!' Lainey gushed. 'Alice, you look amazing! I'm so, so glad you decided to come!'

'Definitely,' Yaz chimed in. 'It's ages since we've hung out. We can have a real girly catch up!'

Erin just rolled her eyes. 'You're the one in the school play, right?' she asked, as if I hadn't been sitting three rows ahead of her in the same form room ever since the start of Year Seven. 'Savvy thinks that's cool.'

Clearly Erin wasn't too impressed that I was there and she wasn't scared to show it. At least she was honest, and I liked that in a way. I knew where I stood with Erin, but Savvy, Lainey and Yaz were acting like I was some kind of royalty, which was unsettling. A couple of weeks back, they wouldn't have even looked at me, let alone bothered to speak; I couldn't work out why things had changed, but I wasn't about to question it too much.

Savvy linked my arm. 'Come on, Alice. I've left my iPhone upstairs, so you and I can take your stuff up to the

bedroom while these guys get on with their face paint. I'll give you the guided tour!'

We wandered through to the kitchen, which was almost as big as the lounge. It was all black granite worktops and spotlights, with a brushed steel range cooker the size of a jeep, and the table was strewn with eggshells and jam, unwashed mixing bowls and used muffin tins. A couple of aprons were draped over a chair and an open recipe book, speckled with flour, lay in one corner. It looked like Lainey, Yaz and Erin had been there all afternoon, baking and not bothering to clear up behind them.

'I'll tidy it later,' Savvy said carelessly. 'Before Mum and Dad get home, anyway.'

I blinked. I had just assumed Savvy's parents would be around, but apparently not. The knowledge that they weren't at home sent a rush of anxiety and adrenalin through my body.

'Where are they?' I asked, as casually as I could.

'Weekend away,' Savvy explained. 'In Cornwall. It's their wedding anniversary or something. Don't worry, my big sister Carina is here. She won't bother us, though.'

'Right,' I said. 'Cool.'

'We've been making stuff for the tea party,' she went on. 'Cupcakes and stuff. We've set it all up in the dining room, but it's a surprise. I'll show you later.'

I took the Tupperware box of jam tarts out of my bag and handed them over, and Savvy prised off the lid and laughed out loud.

'Perfect!' she said. 'We were going to make some, but we couldn't get the pastry right. You're brilliant, Alice! I'm so glad I asked you along!'

Savvy abandoned the jam tarts and pulled me onwards, past the dining room with its door firmly closed and back through to the hallway. We trooped up the stairs to the first landing, and Savvy opened all the bedroom doors so I could see inside. Her parents' room had a king-size bed, the headboard made of shiny wood curved like a sleigh. There was a dressing room where Mrs Hunter's designer dresses hung above a row of glass boxes lit by fairy lights to display Jimmy Choos and skyscraper Kurt Geiger stilt-shoes. I had a very strong impression that Mrs Hunter was nothing at all like my mum, whose favourite footwear was a three-year-old pair of pink fun-fur slippers. There was an en-suite bathroom with shelves full of white, fluffy towels and two guest bedrooms that looked like something from a boutique hotel.

'Your house is amazing,' I said, in awe. 'Like something from a movie or a fairy tale!'

'It's cool, right?' Savvy agreed. 'I guess I take it for granted most of the time.'

'I think it's beautiful!' I breathed, and Savvy seemed pleased by my enthusiasm.

'Me and Carina are on the top floor,' she said as we climbed another flight of stairs. 'We have the whole floor to ourselves, and Carina will be going out later, so at least we won't have to listen to her racket all night.'

'How old is she?' I asked.

'Seventeen,' Savvy told me. 'But she thinks she knows everything. She's *so* annoying.'

'I only have a little brother,' I said.

'Lucky you.'

R&B music turned to full volume was pounding out of one of the bedrooms; Savvy just shook her head despairingly and opened the door next to it. Her room was stunning; a queen-size bed with a canopy made from purple sari fabric shot through with silver, an antique dressing table, a clothes rail hung with dozens of tops and dresses and jeans, a cream carpet that your feet just sank into as you walked. There was a whole wall collaged with photos of Savvy and her friends and family doing cool things: Savvy in the south of France as a small child; Savvy with her cousins in New York and Vermont; Savvy with her family at Glastonbury Festival; Savvy pictured with various celebrities, not looking even the tiniest bit starstruck. I kid you not, she'd met Emma Watson and Harry Styles and a whole heap of others. Her dad's best friend was a photographer and Savvy had clearly hung around a few celebrity shoots. There were tons of photos of Savvy, Erin, Lainey and Yaz doing fun stuff, too: ice skating, eating pizza, lounging in onesies, wearing bikinis and sunglasses on some beach.

A hundred different versions of a perfect friendship. I couldn't quite see where I might fit in, although I knew that Lainey and Yaz had only been part of this golden circle for eighteen months. The picture wall showed glimpses of friendships past, smiling childish faces now relegated to the sidelines. It seemed that Savvy changed her friends as regularly as her hairstyle.

I was sure I recognized a shot of a much younger Savvy

with a girl who looked very much like Serena; I hadn't realized till now that her comments about Savvy might have been made from personal experience.

'I didn't know you'd been friends with Serena,' I said. 'Cool.'

Savvy wrinkled up her nose. 'Serena?' she echoed. 'I don't think so. I don't know anyone called Serena!'

I pointed to the photograph, and Savvy rolled her eyes, laughing.

'Oh, that Serena!' she laughed. 'Yes, she was in my ballet class when we were seven or eight. We were really close for a couple of months, but I haven't seen her since then. I wonder what happened to her?'

'She's in our class at St Elizabeth's,' I said, incredulous. 'Serena Tait. You must have noticed her!'

'Frizzy hair and spots?' Savvy puzzled.

'Yes, and brilliant at science,' I confirmed. 'You really didn't recognize her?'

Savvy shrugged, careless again. 'It was a long time ago. We'll take some cool pictures later, though – you'll be up there on the picture wall too, Alice. Tonight is going to be so much fun!'

I put my bag down next to the bed and fluffed out my skirt, peering into the dressing table mirror, and then Savvy was beside me, iPhone in her hand, arm outstretched. 'Smile,' she instructed. 'Strike a pose!'

I leaned against Savvy, smiling, then held my hands up, fingers spread wide, pulling a mock-surprised face as Savvy pouted and posed at my side. I caught a glimpse of us in the mirror; Savvy and her new friend, the looking-glass girl.

19

The Bandstand, Carrow Park, Ardenley

The girls sit on the bandstand steps in the thin spring sunshine, subdued and melancholy.

'You should have seen her,' Savvy says. 'She looks terrible, I swear. She's this awful grey colour, like cold porridge. And there's a huge scar like a half-moon on her cheek, from the glass vase. I am not kidding, she looks half dead.'

'Don't say that,' Yaz protests.

'It's true, though,' Savvy insists. 'It's horrible; she just lies there, like . . . well, like she's already dead. Like a shell of a person. And I had to talk to her and pretend she could hear me, but I don't think she could. It was like there was nothing there, nothing at all.' She leans back against the steps, hugging her knees, forlorn.

'So she's actually brain-dead?' Erin wants to know. 'Seriously?'

Savvy shrugs. 'They say not, but I don't think they actually know. It was horrible, Erin. The most horrible thing I've ever had to do!'

Tears well up in Savvy's eyes and slide soundlessly down her cheeks, and Lainey puts an arm around her shoulders and tells her she's amazing and brave and kind for going to visit.

'Amazing and brave?' Savvy echoes. 'I don't think so. Terrified, more like. Sick with guilt. Do you know why I went to see her?'

'Because you care,' Yaz says.

'Because I had to know,' Savvy corrects her. 'I had to know how bad it was; and it is bad, Yaz – it's really, really bad.'

'She'll be OK,' Lainey says hopefully. 'Hospitals always make things look worse than they are.'

Savvy stands up abruptly, kicking against the bandstand wall so a splinter of paint flakes away on the tip of her shoe.

She looks angry enough to tear the whole building down, one kick at a time.

'Don't you get it?' she growls. 'This is serious, Lainey! It can't *be* any worse than it actually is. She's in the ICU, being kept alive by machines. It was awful going in there, but I had to do it. I had to say sorry, and you should say it too. She might *die*!'

An elderly man walking past with his dog glances at them, disapproving, and the girls exchange uneasy glances.

'Shhh!' Lainey whispers. 'What're you trying to do, get us arrested?'

Savvy seems to crumple, sinking down on to the steps again. She rests her head back against the bandstand and the breeze blows wisps of caramel-coloured hair across her damp cheeks.

'Why on earth did you say sorry?' Erin asks. 'You didn't do anything!'

'I did,' Savvy snuffles. 'We all did, but I feel responsible . . .'

'Savvy, that's crazy,' Yaz says. 'It wasn't your fault and it wasn't Lainey's either. If you start apologizing, everyone

will be asking questions and sniffing around. We could be in real trouble!'

'Nobody heard me say it,' Savvy says, whispers. 'Not even Alice. I wish they had!'

'Savvy,' Erin says, patiently. 'I know you feel bad. We all do, but this was an accident!'

'Yes, but . . .'

'But nothing,' Lainey insists. 'We didn't make her fall. OK, maybe we should have been honest about it from the beginning, but we weren't – we panicked. That's not a crime, is it? We decided not to tell the whole truth, but that doesn't change what happened, or make it our fault. If we start changing our story now it'll look really dodgy; you have to see that!'

'Lainey's right,' Yaz says. 'We have to stick to our story. If one of us starts telling the truth, the rest of us will be in trouble . . . and for what? We're all sorry for what happened, we all wish she was well again, but we have to stick to what we said to the police that night, or they'll think we were covering up something bad! Agreed?'

'Agreed,' Erin says, handing her friend a tissue. 'Don't mess up now, Savvy. It won't help Alice!'

Savvy blots her eyes with the tissue, but the tears keep coming.

20

Alice

'Hey, Sweetie, it's Mum. Guess what; I've got some get well cards for you! There's one from Auntie Jan and Uncle Pete, one from Auntie Lou and even one from Elaine and Yaz. I suppose they must be feeling bad. Well, anyway. It's a very nice card, one of those big ones with two cartoon teddy bears on the front; I expect they thought it might make you smile. I wish you'd wake up and smile at me, Alice. I really wish you would . . .'

They are standing under a tree, arms wrapped around each other, so still they look like waxworks. They are big and clumsy-looking, funny old men dressed as schoolboys. I know who they are straight away;

Tweedledum and Tweedledee. They smile and stick their free hands out towards me in greeting.

'We should shake hands,' one of them says. 'It's traditional. But it doesn't mean that we can be friends, not nohow.'

'Contrariwise,' the other corrects. 'It does mean that. And we're not friends, are we? We don't know each other at all.'

The hands are withdrawn hastily and hidden behind their backs.

'I think I do know you,' I say, frowning, because there is something strangely familiar about the situation. 'I think we were friends, once, somehow . . .'

The pair shake their heads. 'No, not nohow,' the first one says.

'Contrariwise,' the other states. 'We may have been friends, once. But friends aren't always forever, you know. We should shake hands, start over!'

They offer their hands again, and, not knowing which to take first, I take them both. Instead of shaking hands, I find myself in the middle of a dance, the three of us circling round and round, going nowhere, until my head is reeling and the ground shifts beneath my feet, and I fall down all over again.

Sleepover

The others appeared in the doorway of Savvy's room, piled inside and started arranging sleeping bags and duvets and pillows on the thick, plush carpet.

'You can put your sleeping bag here,' Lainey said. 'Next to me!'

Savvy switched her iPod on just as I was spreading out my sleeping bag, and I recognized the song at once.

'Oh, Avril Lavigne,' I said. 'This was the theme tune to *Alice in Wonderland*, right? The one with Johnny Depp. It's awesome; I don't know which I love best, the film or the song! It's on my iPod, too.'

'You have such good taste, Alice,' Savvy told me. 'I don't know why it's taken me so long to get to know you!'

Yaz, Lainey and Erin smiled thinly, like the overload of sugary compliments from Savvy was melting their teeth. I pretended not to notice. If Savvy was a little over-the-top friendly, so what? It was better than being invisible.

'We should go tidy that kitchen,' Lainey said, checking her watch. 'It's past seven now; we'd better get a move on!'

'Why?' I asked. 'What's happening?'

Lainey just grinned and said I'd soon see.

'Tidy-up time,' Savvy announced, picking up her iPod. 'We'll all pitch in and blitz it!' She grabbed my hand and pulled me out of there, the two of us laughing.

'Alice (Underground)' played on repeat as we washed the dishes and scrubbed the table and swept the floor; to get us in the mood, Savvy said. It did. Savvy started dancing first, waving a damp tea towel around in the air, wiggling her bum, strutting her stuff. One by one she took our hands and drew us in: first Erin, then Lainey, then Yaz, then me, until the whole lot of us were dancing around the kitchen with tea towels and brooms and pan-scrubbers. I had a dishcloth in one hand and Erin was waving an egg whisk in the air, still soapy from the washing-up bowl, and if there had been any frostiness towards me before, it vanished then. It was impossible to dance around with an egg whisk in your hand and keep a straight face.

'You can dance, too,' Savvy said, and Erin laughed and pretended to chase me around the table with the broom, and overall it was the most fun tidying a kitchen I had ever had.

By eight o'clock, the kitchen was sparkling, and Carina, Savvy's sister, came in, all dressed up in wedge-heeled boots and a little black dress that looked like it had been sprayed on. She was wearing so much make-up there was an orange tidemark around her jawline where the foundation ended, and her false eyelashes were so thick they looked like she'd stuck spiders on her eyelids.

She looked like Savvy, but without the sparkly charm; her expression was bored, uninterested.

'So, I'm going out,' she said. 'You'll be OK, right?'

'We'll be fine,' Savvy said. 'We're not babies, Carina!'

'Whatever,' she said. 'Just behave. Don't do anything stupid.'

'As if,' Savvy said.

Carina shrugged on a little jacket, tucked her handbag under her arm. 'I won't be late back. Not too late, anyway.'

She walked away, leaving a cloud of perfume in her wake. We heard the front door slam behind her, and Savvy threw her head back and laughed. 'Finally!' she said. 'I thought she'd never go! Look, Alice, let me show you what we've set up!'

Someone came up behind me and whipped a clean tea

towel around my eyes like a blindfold. 'Surprise,' Lainey said, as the fabric tightened and was knotted gently behind my head. 'Trust us!'

I wasn't sure if I did, but I wanted to.

Hands whirled me round in a circle – once, twice, three times – until I couldn't tell which way I was facing. Cool fingers touched my elbow, guiding me forward. My heart thumped as I stumbled along the hallway, my fingertips stretched out before me, my mouth stretched into a smile.

'This way,' Savvy's voice sang out ahead, and I heard the sound of a door opening and allowed myself to be led inside, my heels clipping sharply against a wooden floor.

'She's a good sport, at least,' Erin commented.

'Blindfold off,' Savvy instructed. 'Let her see now!'

I blinked and looked around.

The dining room was decorated with balloons and bunting. I could see Savvy arranging the jam tarts I'd brought on a fancy cake stand; all along the table there were plates heaped with beautifully decorated cupcakes, plates of quiche and triangular sandwiches with the crusts cut off.

A big teapot with hearts and polka dots sat in the middle of the table, a label saying 'drink me' tied to the handle, and mismatched side plates and cups and saucers were set out in front of every chair. Playing cards were scattered across the tablecloth, along with red and white roses that must have cost a fortune.

'What do you think, Alice?' Savvy asked me. 'Do you like it?'

My eyes shone. 'I must be in Wonderland,' I said.

'Just you wait,' Savvy said. 'This is just the start of it. Lainey, can you send that text?'

Lainey smiled and tapped out a message on her mobile; a moment later a reply bleeped through.

'Sorted,' she said, grinning. 'They're on their way.'

'Who are?' I asked, confused. 'What's happening?'

'Some friends,' Savvy said, evasively. 'Just a little get together. Don't worry, Alice, you'll like it!'

My happiness evaporated, replaced by uncertainty, anxiety. I wasn't sure I would like it, not at all.

21

The Copper Kettle Cafe, Ardenley

Savvy toys with a strawberry milkshake, listless, sad-eyed.

'You were so brave to go and visit,' Erin says. 'I know I couldn't have. Hospitals creep me out. No wonder you're all upset, Savvy.'

'Her mum asked me if I'd come back,' Savvy says. 'Talk to her. The doctors think that hearing her friends talking to her might help. How do you think that made me feel? I wasn't really her friend, was I? None of us were!'

'She was a loner,' Lainey says. 'That's not our fault.'

'But you were friends with her once, weren't you?' Savvy points out. 'In primary school? What went wrong?'

Yaz launches into a spiel about how Alice was given a lead role in the school play in Year Six and suddenly thought she was better than everyone else, but Savvy doesn't look convinced.

'She must have changed a lot, then,' Erin says. 'She's never seemed that way at school, and she didn't strike me that way on Saturday; not at all. I actually liked her. She was fun.'

'She was great,' Lainey agrees, taking her cue from Erin. 'She probably has changed a bit. Grown up, you know? I think maybe we could have been friends again, if this hadn't happened.'

'We're talking about her like she's dead,' Savvy snaps. 'She's not – but she's really, really ill. I keep having these awful nightmares where she dies and comes back to haunt me and tells me it's all my fault . . .'

'She won't die,' Lainey says.

'You don't know that,' Savvy snaps. 'You haven't seen her; how ill she looks. Those machines are keeping her alive, and all because I invited her to a stupid sleepover.'

'You were trying to be nice,' Erin says.

'Yeah, right. We all know that wasn't the reason I asked

her,' Savvy says. 'We used her; tricked her. Why don't we just say it like it is?'

The girls shift in their seats, sipping their drinks, touching up their lipgloss, checking their phones. The truth curls around them like a bad smell, but they pretend not to notice. Talking about it is too difficult, too shameful.

'I might go and see her at the hospital, then,' Yaz says into an awkward silence. 'If you think it would help?'

'It might,' Savvy says. 'You could talk about old times, happy memories. Maybe you can pull her back into the real world?'

'I'll visit too,' Lainey offers. 'For old times' sake.'

Savvy pushes her glass away, the milkshake only half drunk.

'Be prepared for a shock,' she tells them. 'She's linked up to all these drips and wires and they had to cut her hair off for the operation. Her lovely long hair. I felt like crying when I saw her!'

'That's awful,' Yaz says.

'So sad,' Erin agrees.

Savvy's eyes grow wide. 'Has anyone told Luke?' she asks.

'He might not know! I mean, they were old friends, once, weren't they? And there was a bit of a thing going on between them the other night, definitely. Someone should speak to him. Maybe he'd like to visit?'

Lainey finishes the last of her milkshake, scooping up the remaining froth with the end of her straw.

'I've got his number,' she says. 'I'll sort it. No worries.'

22

Alice

*'Hello, Alice, it's me again, Sister Fitzgerald. I'm just going to give
you a quick wash, and change your dressings for when your visitors
come, and I need to change your feeding tube too. It doesn't look too
appetizing, this soupy, liquid stuff they're giving you. You should
give the hospital food a whirl; it's not bad! Y'know what, Alice?
When you wake up I'll make sure you get a feast. You can order
anything you like. What would you pick? Roast turkey, or nachos
with cheese and sour cream and jalapenos, or a big pizza with
every kind of topping? Apple pie and ice cream or red velvet
chocolate cake? Just tell me. And I'll toast you, Alice, with a glass
of champagne – or maybe lemonade, because this is the NHS we're*

talking about, after all. Wake up soon, Alice. There are a lot of people missing you.'

I'm not sure how I got here. It's dark, a kind of hallway with doors all around it, and there's a funny little three-legged table with a bottle on it. The bottle has a label with 'drink me' printed on it in large letters.

It would be silly to drink it just because of the label, of course. It could be poison, or some nasty, foul-tasting medicine, left here as a joke. I pick it up and look at it carefully, then uncork the top and breathe in the aroma. I don't think it's poison. I'm pretty sure it's not.

I take a sip, and it tastes like cherry tart, custard, pineapple, roast turkey, toffee and hot buttered toast. And just as I am think-ing that it's the best thing I have ever tasted, I feel myself shrinking, getting smaller and smaller, until there's barely anything left of me at all.

Sleepover

Savvy picked up the teapot and poured fizzy pink liquid into a vintage teacup.

'Wonderland starts here,' she told me. 'We made some fruit punch earlier. Try it, Alice! It's gorgeous! I put a whole handful of mushed-up strawberries in there!'

I took the teacup and saucer, obedient; a handwritten label saying 'drink me' was tied to the bone china handle. I lifted the cup and drank, sipping cold, fizzy liquid that tasted of fruit and sugar with something bitter and burny hidden beneath it.

'What is that?' I spluttered. 'Alcohol?'

'No, no, nothing like that,' Savvy laughed. 'It's just lemonade, really, but we were experimenting a bit. There might be some bitter lemon in it. And possibly a dash of chilli sauce . . .'

I wasn't stupid – I knew that bitter lemon, strawberries and chilli sauce were not supposed to smell this way; like a brewery, like the whiff of Dad's hot, sour breath the morning after Uncle Jim's stag party. I was sure Savvy was lying, but I pretended not to care. She poured out more of the punch and handed teacups to Erin, Yaz and Lainey. All four of them knocked back their drinks eagerly, pulling faces at the nasty taste, giggling like it was no big deal.

'Oof; pretty strong,' Erin said with a smirk. 'Tastes rank . . .'

'It'll do the job,' Savvy said. 'Drink up, Alice! Don't be a wuss!'

I didn't want to be a wuss, but I didn't want to drink the fruit punch either. I was certain it contained a generous slug of something stolen from Savvy's parents' drinks cabinet, diluted with lemonade and strawberries and half a ton of sugar.

I took another sip and my throat burned; my whole body felt warm and glowy. What happened in *Alice in Wonderland* when she drank the magic potion? She shrank right down to a few inches tall and stepped through a tiny doorway into a different world. In the book, the potion tastes of cherry tart and custard and hot buttered toast and a bunch of other things all mixed up; I was worried this drink was a bit more like the one the White Queen makes in the film – from worm fat, the urine of a horsefly, three coins from a dead man's pocket and two teaspoons of wishful thinking.

Well, more than two teaspoons of wishful thinking, really. There was a whole bucketful of that swishing around inside me already. Wishful thinking was why I was there, wanting to fit in, to be a part of Savvy's world, to have my old friends back. I just wasn't sure that Savvy's weird cocktail was the answer. A part of me thought that if I drank it, I might be transformed somehow, accepted. Another part knew that this was not a ticket to Wonderland, but to some other place; somewhere nightmarish, surreal, where I might shrink away, becoming smaller and smaller until there was nothing left of me at all.

'Like it?' Savvy enquired, watching me carefully. 'There might be just the tiniest shot of rum in there; just enough to loosen us up, chill us out!'

'It's great,' I said, trying not to cough. 'Well, not exactly great, but . . . interesting.'

'You're interesting, Alice,' she declared. 'I had you down as an uptight goody-two-shoes, but I think there's much more to you than meets the eye . . .'

I smiled, pathetically pleased to be described as interesting, but not pleased enough to finish the punch. I spotted a potted plant on a tall stand by the door and wondered if I could get near enough to pour my drink into that, but Savvy was at my side, an arm snaked around my waist.

'Just drink it,' she said, sweetly. 'Knock it back; it's the easiest way. It tastes disgusting, I know, but it will make you feel lovely, I promise! Just all relaxed and happy!'

'I don't really drink,' I confessed as carelessly as I could. 'It's not my thing.'

Was it anybody's thing? We were thirteen years old. Surely that was way too young to drink cocktails of rum and lemonade and strawberries with chilli sauce mixed in? I couldn't imagine wanting to drink something like that at any age. It reminded me of the games I played with Lainey when we were really little, mixing up garden soups and stews for our teddy bears and dolls from mud and grass clippings and flower petals and rainwater.

Lainey was watching me, waiting to see what I'd do. Did she remember those garden brews too?

'None of us really drink,' Savvy said, laughing. 'It's just for fun; part of the Alice theme. Don't wimp out on us.'

It was a tipping point, I knew. I could stay a victim, a loner; or I could take a risk and change everything.

I was still trying to decide whether I had the guts to drink it when the doorbell rang three times.

It was like an alarm bell going off: the girls went all wide-eyed and giggly, smoothing their hair and checking their cute little painted-on noses in the mirror above the sideboard. The doorbell rang again, but nobody seemed to want to actually answer it.

'Who is that?' I asked.

'Our special guests, of course,' Savvy said, laughing. 'You didn't think I'd gone to all this trouble just for us, did you?'

I had thought exactly that, of course, but now that I looked properly I could see that the dining table was set for a crowd, and that the plates heaped high with cupcakes, sandwiches, crisps and pizza held way too much food for just the five of us. I was invisible briefly in the sudden chaos of giggles and mirror-checking, and I drifted over to the big bay window, hiding the punch-filled teacup out of sight behind the heavy brocade curtain. Peeking out of the window from behind the curtain, I glimpsed a bunch of huddled figures clowning around on the path by the door and heard loud chat and whoops of boyish laughter. A pale face flashed out of the darkness briefly, grinning and pushing back an over-grown tawny fringe.

The face was familiar. I knew it well from primary school, from rehearsals for the school play, from that lost summer between primary and secondary school when I went to drama summer school. He was younger then, of course, his face chubbier, cheekier, but even so, I'd have known Luke Miller anywhere.

23

Number 63 bus from Leamington Spa to Ardenley

Luke is coming home from the drama class he takes on a Wednesday evening in Leamington Spa. The class is a long bus ride away but it's worth it to be with other kids who love acting; sometimes they just do improvisation and character studies, but soon the teachers are planning to get them working on a play.

Luke had told Alice about the class at Savvy's on Saturday, and she'd said it sounded great. He'd told her the date, the time, the place; asked if she'd come along. Alice said she might just do that.

He'd tapped her number into his mobile at the party, but

♡ ♥ ♠ ♡ ♦ ♣ ♡ ♥ ♠ ♡ ♦ ♣ ♡

although he's texted her a few times since Saturday (OK, more than a few), she still hasn't replied. He half hoped she might show up at tonight's drama class, but of course she didn't.

He takes out his mobile to check again, because he is a sucker for punishment and he can't quite believe, after what happened at Savvy's, that Alice can be blanking him now. Predictably, there are no new messages. It doesn't make sense. Was she playing games? He expects that kind of thing from girls like Savvy – the popular, confident, princessy kind of girls; but he'd been sure Alice was different.

Then again, he'd given her his landline number back when drama club ended and waited for her to call; she never did.

Suddenly, his mobile begins to buzz with an incoming call; the name Lainey flashes up on the screen. Luke presses the screen to take the call.

'Hello, Luke,' Lainey says. 'I thought I should ring. The thing is – well, it's about Alice . . .'

'What about Alice?' he asks.

'Look, I can't really explain over the phone,' Lainey

says. 'We need to talk; I could meet you tonight, if you're not busy, or tomorrow. At the Copper Kettle Cafe, or the park – anywhere, really. And I can explain properly.'

Luke frowns, his mind working overtime.

'Has she changed her mind?' he asks. 'I wondered why she wasn't returning my texts or answering my calls. If she doesn't want to talk to me, she just has to say; she doesn't have to send a go-between!'

'It's not quite that simple,' Lainey whispers. 'I'm not her go-between. I can't explain over the phone. Will you meet me?'

'Look, I don't like game-playing,' he says. 'This is ridiculous. Why can't Alice talk to me herself?'

'She can't,' Lainey insists. 'You'll understand when I see you and explain. It's important, Luke, I promise. I need to talk to you. Tomorrow?'

'I guess,' Luke says with a sigh. 'Ten o'clock at the cafe, then?'

'Perfect,' Lainey says. 'I'll tell you everything then; I swear.'

Luke doesn't understand what's going on, but he doesn't

have Alice's address or home phone number. He wants some answers, and right now Lainey is his only chance of getting them.

24

Alice

'Hello, Alice, it's Dr Fleet. I'm working with some medical students today, and I'm hoping you won't object if they help with the routine tests and checks. So, everybody, gather round: this is Alice, who had a very nasty fall on Saturday night. We've set some broken bones in her arm and operated to stop a bleed in the cerebral cortex, but she hasn't come round yet. Don't you worry, Alice, we plan to fix you up and ship you out of here just as soon as we can; you just have to wake up for us, OK?'

If you have never tried to play croquet with a flamingo, I do not recommend it; the flamingo keeps twisting round to look me in the face, and when I do manage to get it to straighten its neck I find that the

croquet ball, which seems to be a hedgehog, has got up and walked
away. I can't say I blame it.

I am not the only one struggling; the garden is filled with party
guests: kings, queens, knaves – even the White Rabbit. If you add
assorted flamingoes, hedgehogs and playing-card soldiers into the mix,
it is a kind of chaos. It makes my head ache.

The Queen of Hearts appears in the distance, her face like thunder.
She scans the crowds, her eyes coming to rest on me.

'Off with her head!' she roars. 'Off with her head!'

Sleepover

Savvy answered the door and the boys swarmed into the
hallway; laughing, talking, clowning around. There were
five of them and five of us; I saw at once that this had been
planned, and wondered if I had been invited to somehow
make up the numbers.

I didn't have time to worry or even care – I was there,
and that was what mattered.

The only one of the boys who'd bothered to dress up
was Luke. Just like in the primary school play, he was
the Mad Hatter, grinning in a tall top hat with a label

saying '10/6d' tucked into its crimson band. He didn't see me at first, because Lainey had taken him by the hand, introducing him to Erin. 'I'm charmed!' he said, taking his hat off and bowing low, and although it was a cheesy gesture it was somehow cool too. It made everyone laugh.

'Savvy you met the other weekend,' Lainey reminded him. 'And you'll remember Alice and Yaz from primary school, of course,' Lainey went on. 'Right?'

'Of course,' Luke said, but his eyes slid over Savvy and Yaz and fixed on me, and it was like he was looking right into my soul. I could feel my cheeks burning; my heart thumped so hard I was surprised it wasn't visible through the soft blue cotton of my dress.

Luke Miller was taller than I remembered, his shoulders broader, his face more angular; but his hair was still a tumble of unruly waves and his eyes were still the same dark blue. The boy I'd had a secret crush on the summer after Year Six was just plain gorgeous now.

I wanted to turn and run away, find the nearest rabbit hole and fling myself down it. I didn't, though. I stood my ground and acted like I wasn't terrified. I tilted my

chin up and smiled at Luke, pretending I was confident, calm, cool.

'Hey, Alice,' he said. 'Long time no see.'

'Hi, Luke. Or should I say Hatter?'

His face broke into the hugest grin, and he raised an eyebrow, teasingly. 'So tell me, Alice,' he said. 'Why is a raven like a writing desk?'

It was an old in-joke we'd once shared – a line from the play – and as he spoke it the awkwardness and embarrassment I'd been feeling peeled away. This was Luke, just Luke, who had been a good friend to me that long-ago summer when Lainey and Yaz were going cold on me and drifting away.

Time can change people, I knew that, but I wasn't sure it had changed Luke.

'So, these are my friends; Robbie Sharp and Dex Robbins and Josh Brown and Kamil Akan,' he said, and the boys behind him grinned and waggled their fingers in greeting. 'You did say we should just drop in, Savvy, so we did!'

'Awesome,' Savvy said. 'Alice – Lainey and I were in town a couple of weeks back and we just happened to bump into

Luke and Dex. I mean, we were literally just in the same cafe grabbing a drink, and Lainey recognized Luke, and we all got talking.'

'Cool,' I said lamely, watching the way Savvy's eyes lingered on Dex, who was one of those boy-band looka-likes with fair tousled hair and soft brown eyes. 'Really cool.'

'We all got on soooo well,' Savvy explained, carelessly. 'Didn't we, Dex? I was telling Luke and Dex that we St Elizabeth's girls don't get to hang out with boys much these days, being at an all-girls school and everything.'

'So we decided to get together again, with a few new faces thrown into the mix, and here we are,' Lainey finished. 'Luke and I were mates back in primary, of course . . .'

I wasn't sure that Lainey and Luke had actually even spoken to each other at primary school, in spite of her mad crush, but still she placed her hand on his arm as if laying claim. I thought for a moment he might brush her away, but Luke was too polite for that; still laughing, he allowed himself to be pulled forward, towards the dining room, the other boys following in his wake. When Savvy threw open

the door to reveal the Alice-themed spread, they all whistled and laughed and piled in, eyeing the food as if they hadn't eaten in a week.

The big teapot sat abandoned on the sideboard, but a big cut-glass punchbowl was in the centre of the table, filled with a fruity, fizzy mixture. A label saying 'drink me' was tied to the handle of the ladle Erin was using to fill everyone's teacups.

Savvy touched my arm as I hesitated in the doorway.

'Don't worry, Alice,' she whispered. 'That one really is fruit punch, I promise. The teapot brew was just for us; I thought we might need a bit of a confidence boost with the boys around. I know I did, anyway. OK?'

'OK,' I said, relieved that there'd be no more of the eye-watering rum mixture and amazed that someone like Savvy might need a confidence boost to hang out with a few boys. I had imagined her to be perfect, but the more I saw of her the more she seemed just perfectly imperfect, with strengths and weaknesses the same as everyone else.

Savvy sat at the head of the table with Dex next to her. The rest of us sat down awkwardly, wherever there was a

spare chair. Luke was about to flop down next to me when Lainey tugged his arm and pulled him round to the other side of the table. He looked at me from behind a towering three-tier cake stand piled high with cupcakes, and I thought I saw him mouth a silent apology at me; maybe it was just wishful thinking.

The boy called Kamil sat down next to me and leaned across to tell me that I reminded him of Keira Knightley, which was so ridiculous I couldn't think of a single thing to say. I just raised one eyebrow, too polite to suggest he find a slightly less bizarre chat-up line; he turned away at once, deflated, to talk to Erin instead. I could hear him asking if anyone had ever told her she looked like Shakira, and she snorted and asked him if anyone had ever told him he needed an eye test, and then a stony silence descended over our corner of the table.

The others were in flirt mode; chatting brightly, offering sandwiches and 'eat me' cupcakes around the table, but it was still kind of awkward. We were five slightly tipsy teenage girls who weren't used to having boys around, trying to make small talk and not quite succeeding. We were in fancy dress and the boys weren't, apart

from Luke with his vintage top hat. It all seemed too contrived, like some kind of ill-advised multiple blind date with zero chemistry.

'D'you like football?' Kamil tried again, a note of desperation in his voice. 'I support Chelsea. I used to live in London, y'see.'

'My little brother supports Aston Villa,' I said politely, but it was a mistake. Kamil was off on a rant about the Premier League and I picked up an 'eat me' cake and nibbled absently at the icing, wishing it really could make me taller or smaller; anything to escape the ear-bleeding dullness.

Luke grinned at me across the table and mimed a yawn, and that made me smile.

Once we'd eaten, the chat stalled again, but of course, Savvy had a fallback plan. She put on a CD and announced we'd be playing some party games. I was pretty sure that thirteen was too old to play pass the parcel and musical chairs – the kind of games Lainey, Yaz and I had played years ago at birthday parties in draughty church halls or crammed living rooms – but Savvy had something different in mind, of course.

'Let's do a bit of truth or dare,' she said. 'We all have to confess to some dark secret nobody else knows, or do a dare of my choosing. So – tell me, what's the naughtiest thing you ever did as a child?'

The ice began to melt, slowly at first, then faster. Savvy went round the table in turn. Erin confessed that she'd switched the labels on Christmas presents under the tree because she had wanted the chemistry set she knew her brother was getting; Lainey admitted she'd scratched the paintwork on her mum's boyfriend's car with a nail because he'd yelled at her; Yaz said she'd buried a brand new pair of school shoes at the bottom of the garden because she hated them so much, and nobody had ever found out; Josh wouldn't confess to anything, and Savvy made him stand on a chair and sing 'It's Raining Men', while we gave him marks out of ten, *X Factor* style.

Everyone was screeching with laughter by the time it was Luke's turn, and he looked right at me across the tiered cake stand and confessed how, back in primary school, he'd once deliberately tripped up a girl he really liked, making her drop a dish of rice pudding all over the dining room floor.

'What did you do that for, if you fancied her, idiot?' Kamil wanted to know.

'I wanted her to notice me,' he said with a shrug.

'And did she?'

'No. She kicked me in the shins and didn't speak to me for the next three years,' Luke admitted.

His eyes hooked on to mine again, and I couldn't look away, even though my cheeks had flared scarlet. I knew Luke's story already, because I'd been in it.

I was the girl.

25

The Copper Kettle Cafe, Ardenley, Thursday

'Thanks for coming to meet me,' Lainey says. 'There's something serious I have to tell you, Luke. Something terrible. When I spoke to you last night I realized you hadn't heard, and maybe I'm a coward, but I just couldn't tell you on the phone. Oh God, it's too awful!'

Lainey's eyes brim with tears, and Luke feels the first stirrings of panic. This is not going to be a conversation about whether Alice wants to see him again; it's something else entirely. Something really bad.

'What is?' he demands. 'What are you talking about?'

'Luke, there was an accident. At Savvy's. After you and the others left.'

The skin on Luke's neck prickles with fear.

'Accident?' he echoes. 'What accident?'

Lainey starts talking then, about how they were all asleep at one in the morning when they were woken by an almighty crash. The girls stumbled out on to the landing to find that Alice had fallen from the first floor landing right down the stairs to the bottom. She had hit her head on the tiled floor and pulled down a glass vase of roses and a big mirror which had shattered and cut her face, and they'd had to call an ambulance in the middle of the night. Alice had been in hospital ever since.

'Hang on,' Luke interrupts, distraught. 'How did she fall? What happened? Is she OK?'

Lainey wipes her eyes. 'Not really,' she says. 'Alice is really ill; she hasn't regained consciousness. I mean, it's awful for Alice, obviously, but it's traumatic for the rest of us too, because we found her. It was terrible, Luke. I'll never forget it. I thought she was dead!'

Luke puts a hand on Lainey's arm, as much to steady himself as anything else.

'She wasn't,' he says. 'You found her, and you raised the alarm, and hopefully she'll be OK.'

'I hope so,' Lainey whispers. Her eyes are brimming with tears and Luke tries to comfort her because crying girls make him panic a little, but when he tries to take his hand away to find a clean tissue she grabs it and hangs on tight. Her hand is hot and slightly clammy, and her fingernails are digging into his palm a little, but he tries not to notice.

'Look, talking won't help,' he says. 'Shouldn't we be visiting her?'

'Yes, of course,' Lainey gulps. 'I think the visiting starts from midday. We could go together.'

He nods. 'How did she fall? I don't understand.'

Lainey sighs. 'We were all asleep,' she explains. 'Like I told you, it was past one in the morning, and suddenly we woke up to this horrible crashing noise. We ran out on to the landing, and Alice had fallen. It was so scary, Luke!'

'You think she tripped in the dark?' he asks, pulling his hand from her grip. He can see where her fingernails have left pale crescent marks on his skin.

'It wasn't dark,' Lainey corrects him, quickly. 'The landing lights were on. Maybe she just lost her footing. She was

wearing those shoes, and they were quite high for someone who always wears flats.'

Luke frowns. 'Why was she wearing shoes in the middle of the night? When you were all asleep?'

'I don't know. She even had her coat on. I suppose we were wondering if she'd got homesick suddenly and decided to go home.'

Luke rakes a hand through his hair. 'She was pretty bright and lively when we left. And, well, she doesn't seem like the kind of person who'd run away from a sleepover in the middle of the night.'

Lainey sips her hot chocolate and sighs.

'Alice has changed,' she says. 'She's not the girl we knew at primary. Since we started secondary she's been nervy and moody; a bit of a loner. She didn't want to know me or Yaz any more; stopped hanging out with us completely, which was a bit upsetting at the time, but well, there wasn't anything we could do.'

Luke looks troubled, like he's working on a particularly difficult maths problem and something just isn't adding up. He finishes his latte and pushes the mug away.

'Thing is,' he says, 'we didn't leave till past eleven, and

Savvy said you'd be watching DVDs and doing makeovers and girly stuff all night. So how come you were all fast asleep at one in the morning? I mean, seriously, you were all totally hyper when we left. What the heck happened?'

Lainey's face registers panic, and a dark flush of pink stains her cheeks. A tear rolls slowly down her cheek, and she wipes it away with her sleeve.

'Change of plan,' she says. 'We were all tired, and Savvy said the DVDs could wait till morning, so we crashed out. I'd give anything to change that now, Luke. Anything!'

Without warning, she flings her arms around him and hangs on tight, sobbing on his shoulder, and Luke finds himself patting her back awkwardly and whispering words of comfort, over and over.

26

Alice

'Alice? This is Mum. Guess what; your friends are here to see you! Elaine and that nice boy Luke who was in the play with you at primary school. Isn't that lovely? Alice? Can you hear me?'

By the time I stop running, the croquet party is far behind me. I'm in a clearing shaded by trees, and I can hear talking and the clink of china and cutlery. Peering through the trees, I see a table set for a tea party, and the March Hare and Dormouse sipping their drinks.

The Mad Hatter is on his feet, taking off his hat as he sweeps into a low bow. 'Alice!' he exclaims, raking a fall of wavy brown hair

back from his face. 'You made it at last! We've been waiting for you!
Do you remember me?'

The Hatter looks very familiar, but still, I don't remember him. I
wish I did. He seems like someone you'd never want to forget.

Sleepover

The Mad Hatter's Tea Party was a success. Every sandwich
was eaten, every cupcake scoffed, every last scoop of fruit
punch dished up and drunk. Never underestimate the appe-
tite of a teenage boy – or five. By the time we left the table,
abandoning the empty plates, scrunched-up cupcake cases
and crumbs, we had bonded over embarrassing childhood
confessions and drunk enough fizzy punch to be hyper on
sugar and laughter.

Savvy led the way through to the living room, and by
that time she had Dex practically eating out of her hand.
Erin seemed to be getting on well with Robbie, and Yaz
and Josh were bonding over football teams and computer
games. That left Lainey and me with Kamil and Luke.
Kamil looked less than impressed, and Lainey was hanging
on to Luke's arm for dear life, as if he might make a run

for it at any minute. He shot me a long-suffering look, as if he were at least considering it.

Erin put her iPod on shuffle and Yaz opened a big bottle of Coke, in case we weren't wired enough already. Savvy pulled the plush brocade cushions right off the sofa and flung them on the floor, and she sat us down on them in a rough circle: girl, boy, girl, boy. Savvy produced a wine bottle from behind the sofa, and my heart sank – but it wasn't to drink. It was much worse than that.

'Spin the bottle,' she told us. 'You've all heard of it, haven't you?'

I'd heard of it, all right; every teenager's worst nightmare, a game where one person had to spin the bottle and then head off somewhere quiet to kiss whoever the bottle pointed at. I'd never played it, but I'd always thought it sounded like pure torture.

'This is kind of the same,' Savvy was saying. 'Only there's a time limit. My older cousins in America play it; they call it seven minute heaven. It'll be fun!'

I tried to smile, but it turned into more of a grimace.

According to Savvy, the rules were simple. Someone would spin the bottle and wait for it to stop, pointing to

someone of the opposite sex; they'd then get seven minutes alone together. 'To talk,' Savvy explained. 'Break the ice, get to know each other a bit better. Or . . . whatever!'

'I like the sound of "whatever",' Dex joked.

'I bet,' Savvy laughed. 'Anyway, I have a timer, and I'm going to be really strict about it.'

It wasn't strict; it was chaos. The music was thumping and everyone was talking at once. Savvy went first, and the bottle pointed to Josh. The two of them vanished for seven minutes, and the rest of us were supposed to guess the answers to riddles while they were away, but this diversion failed almost at once and Lainey got us all to pose for photos for her Instagram feed instead. I felt anxious, panicky. I remembered the part in *Alice in Wonderland* where Alice found herself drowning in a sea of her own tears, and although I wasn't about to cry in front of a bunch of people I hardly knew, I knew I was way, way out of my depth.

I didn't want to go off into a back room and kiss a random boy I'd never met before, or whatever we were supposed to do. This wasn't my idea of fun at all. If this was a test to see if I was right for Savvy's little posse of friends, I was failing it, big style. My frozen grin betrayed me.

'Hey,' Luke said, nudging my elbow while the others were busy posing and preening for Lainey's iPhone. 'It's been a while, Alice. How come you don't go to drama club any more?'

I blinked. 'I thought it closed,' I said. 'It did, didn't it?'

'It did, but I found another one in Leamington that's just as good,' he told me. 'A few of the old group go; I just assumed everyone knew. You'd like it, Alice. The teachers are great. We put on a summer production every year, and work on some really cool projects in between. It's six till eight on Wednesdays. You should come; seriously!'

My cheeks burned with the pleasure of being remembered, being wanted. It felt like Luke had thrown me a lifeline.

'Maybe I will.'

'Cool! Give me your mobile number and we can meet in town; take the bus together,' Luke went on. 'They'd be glad to have you, I'm sure!'

He took out his mobile and tapped my details into his

contacts list. My mobile was in my coat pocket upstairs, but still, my heart thumped at the idea that he might message me. Maybe one day soon we might be sitting on a bus together, heading for Leamington and drama club, and it would be just like old times, only better.

'Hatter!' Lainey's voice rang out. 'Where are you hiding? I need you in these photos! C'mon, Luke, don't be shy!'

He rolled his eyes and allowed himself to be drawn back into the photoshoot, and I perched on the arm of a chair and watched and tried not to feel sad that nobody called out for me to join in.

When Savvy and Josh came back from their seven minutes, it was his turn to spin the bottle; he ended up with Yaz. So it went on. Yaz ended up with Robbie; Robbie got Savvy; Savvy tugged the rug a bit until she got Dex. Some people got their seven minutes with a bunch of different partners – but I missed out every time. There was a lot of cheating and nudging the bottle and pulling at the rug, but I didn't care. Erin ended up with Kamil and Kamil got Lainey, and Lainey, of course, with a little extra shove of the bottle, picked Luke.

I was surprised at how hurt I felt as the two of them left the room. Lainey had liked Luke for years, I knew that, but still, I felt crushed.

The others were watching some funny YouTube video Josh had on his phone, of dogs trying to sing along to a One Direction song. They'd lost interest in the game. I watched the living room clock; the hands dragged round like they were made of lead, but finally Lainey and Luke came back. Lainey had an arm snaked around his waist and her eyes were shining.

I remembered how back when we were friends she'd always had a knack of getting what she wanted: the best toy, the cutest dress, the biggest ice cream – the one with chocolate flakes and strawberry sauce and sprinkles. Lainey always managed to get it.

And now she had Luke.

'What will we do next, Savvy?' Lainey asked, hanging on to him so he couldn't get away. 'Your hide and seek game? That would be cool!'

'We haven't finished this game yet,' Luke pointed out. 'Don't I get a chance to spin the bottle? It's not fair, otherwise. Everyone should have a go, surely?'

'Sure, whatever!' she said. 'It's just that it's getting late and Savvy wanted to try this team thing.'

'It's a grown up version of hide and seek,' Savvy explained. 'Two teams: boys and girls. To keep the *Alice in Wonderland* theme going I'm going to paint hearts on the girls' cheeks and diamonds on the boys'.'

Lainey was grinning, sure she'd got her own way, but then Savvy spoke again.

'I can do the face-painting while Luke takes his turn,' she said. 'Then we'll call it a day and move on. Anyone who didn't get a go can get first shot in the next game, OK?'

Lainey's face fell, but we sat down again and Luke sent the bottle spinning, and when it slowed and threatened to stall by Lainey, he nudged it with the toe of his Vans deck shoe and the whole bottle skidded across the rug and almost landed right in my lap.

'Cheating,' Lainey accused, her face sour.

'You cheated too, Lainey,' Kamil pointed out. 'Everyone's cheated, pretty much.'

'Kind of fits, too,' Savvy decreed. 'Alice and the Hatter; I like it!'

Lainey didn't like it, though. Her eyes were dark with sadness or anger – I couldn't tell which – and when I shrugged and tried to mouth 'sorry' she turned away.

'Timer's on,' Savvy said. 'Seven minutes, guys.'

Luke jumped up, swept off his hat and bowed low, then took my hand and led me from the room.

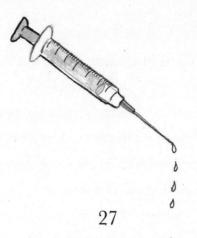

27

ICU, Ardenley General Hospital

'Oh my God,' Lainey says. 'I know they said she was sick, but this is worse than anything I imagined. She looks awful! Like all those tubes and machines are just keeping her alive. I've seen things like this on TV – it's horrible. And sometimes the person never comes round again, and they have to switch off the life support . . .'

'Lainey, shhh,' Luke whispers. 'What if she can hear you? Don't say those things!'

Lainey's eyes fill with tears. 'It's just, well, you know how close we were at primary school. Alice was my best friend. And we haven't always been close just lately, but best friends are forever, right? And now . . . oh, I can't

bear it! Look at her! She's like, just a shell! It's like she's already gone!'

Lainey starts to cry, and Luke puts an arm around her shoulder and offers her a tissue, trying to edge her towards a visitor's chair. To tell the truth, he is just as shocked as Lainey at how sick Alice looks. This is serious.

Once, long ago when all of them were six or so, Luke remembers that Alice had been chasing Lainey and Yaz across the playground in the middle of some game when she'd tripped and fallen so hard she'd torn her navy blue woolly tights and skinned her knees. Luke had stopped his game of football and gone over to help her up, and then Lainey and Yaz had taken over, bringing her across to the playground attendant who'd cleaned her up and splashed on antiseptic and stuck big wads of lint on to Alice's knees with beige sticking plaster.

She had looked so cute with those crudely plastered knees sticking out from the holes in her tights; it was probably around that time that Luke had realized he really liked her, in a gruff, no nonsense, six-year-old kind of way.

This, though; this is way scarier than skinned knees. This makes Luke sick with fear. He doesn't like hospitals at the best of times; the sharp, antiseptic smell of them, the uniformed nurses with serious faces and clipboards filled with ominous information, the machines, the syringes, the too-bright look in the eyes of every visitor.

And Lainey is right; Alice looks terrible. She is deathly white with smudges of mauve beneath her eyes, that big crescent-shaped scar, her cheeks and lips bleached of all colour. She looks like a broken doll.

Lainey is snuggling into him, looking for comfort, but Luke can't find the words to tell her that things will be fine; things don't look fine at all. He takes his arm away before Lainey gets too attached, and the two of them perch on chairs at Alice's bedside.

'What is it they call it?' Lainey is saying. 'When somebody is stuck in a coma for years and years and there's no hope left for them at all? A persistent vegetative state, that's it. Do you think that's what's happened to Alice?'

'Shhh,' Luke says, angry now. 'Lainey, what if she can *hear* you?'

'She can't hear,' Lainey argues. 'You know she can't, Luke. Don't kid yourself. Just look at her! She's like a – well, a vegetable!'

♡ ♥ ♠ ♡ ♦ ♣ ♡ ♥ ♠ ♡ ♦ ♣ ♡

Luke takes Lainey's arm a little too roughly, pulling her to her feet.

'We should go,' he says. 'This isn't working.'

'I know,' Lainey snuffles. 'It's heartbreaking. It's just too cruel. She was my *best friend*. Not now, maybe, but once – and I can't forget that, Luke, not ever!'

He grits his teeth and steers Lainey out of the room into the corridor. 'I'm sorry, Luke. I know we're supposed to pretend she'll get well again, but . . .'

'Shhh, Lainey,' he says. 'Her parents are in the family room right over there. Can you just shut up, please? Have some respect!'

'I do!' Lainey protests. 'I do! I'm just gutted. I had no idea it would be this bad . . .'

'Hang on,' Luke says. 'I've forgotten something. I'll see you down in the lobby in five minutes, OK?'

He propels Lainey out of the ICU and leaves her standing, open mouthed and tearful, on the far side of the double doors. Luke walks back to Alice's room, enters quietly and walks over to the bed. He cannot blame Lainey for her reaction; Alice looks like a broken girl, expertly put back together, but no longer quite whole.

His fingers reach out to touch her hand, cool and bird-like as it lies on the coverlet. The last time he held her hand, Luke thinks, Alice leaned against him so her long hair fell like a curtain between them, softly crimped and smelling of coconut shampoo. Today he can smell nothing but the sharp, chemical smell of disinfectant, and Alice's hair, if it hasn't all been cut off, is hidden beneath a cocoon of bandages.

'Alice?' he whispers. 'Look, I'm sorry about Lainey. She found it all a bit . . . too much. I'll come back tomorrow, on my own, I promise.'

28

Alice

'I'll be back,' Luke promises. 'Hang on in there, Alice. I'll come back tomorrow, like I said. I know that you're lost right now, but I hope you'll come back, too.'

'We've been here before,' the Hatter says, pouring tea. 'Do you remember?'

My head aches with the effort, but I can't seem to dredge up the memory. I would like to remember, though. I really would. I'm sure the Hatter in the book I once read wasn't this young, this smiley. I'm sure he isn't supposed to make my heart race.

'I don't remember,' I admit. 'I don't remember anything!'

'You will,' the Hatter promises. 'You're just a little lost right now, but I'm going to find you, I promise . . .'

I reach out to take the offered teacup, but suddenly someone yanks the tablecloth and everything flies up in the air in a mess of china and cutlery and fabric, as if a hurricane has hit. I'm pulled into the whirlwind too, into the vortex, as if I'm being dragged back up the rabbit hole this time instead of falling down it. And then the hurricane dumps me down again, alone in the woods in the darkness. I can hear the Hatter's promise swirling around my head, but he has gone, and the ache of loneliness in my throat is so sharp I think it might choke me.

A single tear slides out from beneath the lashes of the girl lying motionless in the ICU. The tear slips down her cheek, but the nurses are brisk and busy, checking machines and drips and temperature and blood pressure. Checking for tears is not on their list, and in the half-light of a hectic ICU, nobody sees.

Sleepover

So . . . yeah. Seven minute heaven.

I was beyond embarrassed. I followed Luke into the

shadowy hallway, a few half-hearted wolf-whistles and catcalls following us, my face aflame.

'I hate this,' I said. 'I might as well just tell you now, Luke. It just feels so fake, so cringey. I didn't think people actually acted this way outside American teen movies.'

Luke laughed. 'I don't think they do. Savvy's great, but she's trying a bit too hard . . .'

'All-girls school,' I said. 'We tend to either over-compensate and go wild – that's Savvy – or else just freeze up totally when there are boys around. I fall into the second category, obviously.'

'You don't look frozen to me,' Luke said. 'Spin the bottle is really not my style, but I wanted to talk to *you*, so don't go freezing up on me, Alice Beech. So. How do we get out of here?'

'Out of here?' I echoed. 'I don't think we do . . .'

Luke had other ideas. He spotted the back door, turned the handle and we stepped out on to the darkened patio. I remembered the bit in *Alice in Wonderland* when Alice wants to shrink and step through the tiny door into a magic garden, and wondered if it would have felt this way.

'Where are we going?' I asked.

'Exploring,' Luke said. 'Or maybe escaping. Who cares?'

He took my hand again in the dark and I felt a jolt of pure joy fizz through me. I wanted to throw my head back and laugh at the velvet night sky, the stars that seemed to be shining just for us.

Then I remembered that Luke had just spent seven minutes alone with Lainey, and my heart stopped soaring and sank like a stone. I was an idiot, so easily fooled it was a joke. I pulled my hand away.

'What's up?' he asked.

'Did you have fun with Lainey?' I asked. 'I bet she didn't mind holding hands.'

Luke laughs. 'She didn't mind at all,' he said. 'She practically had me in a headlock. She kissed me, which was flattering, I suppose, but look, Alice, I don't like Lainey; I like you.'

I battled with jealousy, pride and distrust. 'You really don't like Lainey?' I checked. 'Are you sure? Because she seems very keen on you . . .'

He held his hands up in the darkness, grinning. His

169

blue eyes seemed as dark as the sky; brighter than the stars.

'She's a nice girl,' Luke said. 'Friendly . . .'

'Very,' I said.

Luke just laughed. 'You want the truth? It wasn't a good kiss. It was a bit like being pinned down by an overenthusiastic Labrador. Don't tell her I said that . . .'

'I won't,' I said. 'A Labrador? Really?'

'Come on, Alice,' Luke said. 'You know I'm not interested in Lainey, I'm interested in you. We used to be friends, once, and then you dropped right off the radar and vanished. I mean, people do lose touch, right? I wanted to talk, that's all. I've missed you.'

I smiled in the darkness.

I felt stronger, braver, more alive than I had in ages. I wasn't acting, I wasn't playing a part – I felt like the last couple of years had never happened. Shy Alice, quiet Alice, loner Alice – it was like she'd never existed.

Whatever I'd felt about Luke in the summer after Year Six, this was different. Attraction fizzed through me like Savvy's fruit punch, sweet and tangy and unexpected. And

Luke had missed me; that knowledge made my cheeks burn with pleasure.

We were at the bottom of the garden, standing under a huge oak tree that had an old tyre swing hanging from one sturdy branch. I tried to imagine Savvy or her glamorous big sister as kids, shrieking and swinging through the air on the tyre swing, and failed. I ducked away from Luke and walked up to the swing, pushing it a little so that it swayed gently. The rope creaked as though it was waking up after years of being asleep. I felt kind of the same.

'You'd have been up on that swing, a couple of years ago,' Luke teased. 'You had a bit of a tomboy streak then. Remember when you climbed that tree by the junior school playground because Peter Kelly threw Yaz's skipping rope into the branches? You rescued it, too. I was impressed.'

'That was in Year Four,' I remembered. 'I only did it because Yaz was crying. I never did like Peter Kelly.'

'Do you remember the rice pudding day?' he asked, reminding me of his truth or dare revelation from earlier. 'D'you forgive me?'

'I might . . .'

On impulse, I gripped the weatherworn rope and placed a foot on the tyre swing, pulling myself up. The tyre swayed lazily and I closed my eyes and imagined I was nine years old again; the kind of girl who loved life and climbed trees and had the whole world at her feet. The kind of girl I used to be, and wanted to be again.

Luke just laughed and within minutes he'd grabbed the rope and hauled himself up to face me, the tyre swing lurching haphazardly from side to side.

'Is it strong enough to hold us both?' I asked, my voice no more than a whisper. Luke's feet were pressing against mine from either side; his hands were clasped just above mine on the weathered rope, and his face was so close I could feel the warmth of his breath on my cheek and inhale the sharp spearmint smell of his chewing gum. My hair fell like a curtain between us and Luke raised a hand to push it away, his fingers grazing my skin.

He didn't answer my question; I think we both forgot I'd even asked it. The tyre swing steadied, slowed, and the two of us held on, a breath apart, until he moved or I moved and somehow we weren't even a breath apart any more.

29

Luke

Luke has a thing about making playlists. He takes his iPod everywhere with him and has a playlist for every mood. After he'd kissed Alice on Saturday he started thinking about the songs he'd pick for her; he imagined the two of them walking along together, holding hands, sharing one earbud each to listen to the perfect set of songs.

Now, with Alice ill in hospital, the playlist changes. Luke spends hours scrolling through his favourite songs, trying to guess if they'd appeal to Alice. A Robbie Williams song they once learnt in primary school, a Beatles track from the CD Miss Harper used to play on rainy lunchtimes, the Avril Lavigne song they'd all sung at the start of the *Alice in Wonderland* school play; these are songs he can guess at, a part of their shared past. For the rest, he scours his own song lists, a wild, eclectic mash-up of tracks from the past forty or fifty years.

Luke's dad works as a sound engineer for a theatre, but he once worked for a record company. Luke's mum was once in an 80s girl-band called the Crêpe Suzettes; the press photos show a trio of teenage girls with wildly crimped and backcombed hair and lots of ribbons, polka dots and Doc Marten boots. He finds it hard to tally this image with his mum as she is now: a youth counsellor working with troubled children and teenagers. She no longer backcombs her hair or wears polka dots, but the Doc Martens are still part of her trademark look.

Luke grew up listening to a patchwork of weird and wonderful music, and he picks out tracks from this now, things that Alice might like. Lainey calls him three times as the evening goes on, but Luke ignores each call. He knows that Lainey is hurting just as much as he is, but right now he cannot handle her awkward, frightened comments; her conviction that Alice is smashed beyond repair.

Luke cannot let himself think that way.

He remembers the girl he kissed on the tyre swing on Saturday; the two of them holding on tight, swinging softly, balanced on the edge of something like wonder.

It's not possible for that to be wiped away so easily, surely?

He works on the playlist into the early hours, as if keeping himself busy can somehow drag Alice back from the nightmare she has fallen into. By morning he is satisfied; the playlist covers past, present and future. The music says what he cannot, uses imagery and symbolism and sound to cast a net into the abyss Alice has fallen into.

Perhaps, somehow, it can save her.

By 9 a.m., Luke is back at Ardenley General.

He knows it is too early for visiting, but he holds his head high and walks with confidence past reception and down to the lifts, up to the third floor. The corridors are still damp from the morning cleaning and smell strongly of disinfectant. Walking into the ICU is like stepping into a different world; calm, quiet, gentle, removed from the chaos of the outside world.

Luke sees Alice's mum dozing in a chair beside the bed, a discarded paperback novel on her lap. Her hair is mussed and her clothes are crumpled, as if she's been sitting there

all night. She probably has. Functioning on just a few hours' sleep, Luke knows he probably doesn't look a whole lot better.

'Luke?' Laura Beech says. 'What are you doing here?'

'Hello, Mrs Beech,' he says. 'I hope you don't mind – I made a playlist for Alice. You said that perhaps she can hear us, so I thought she might like some music to listen to. I don't know. I thought that music might reach her even if words can't.'

Luke's eyes slide towards the bed, where Alice is still, silent. A tide of anger rushes through his body; he wants to pull out the tubes and wires attached to her, rip away the bandages that swathe her head. He doesn't, of course. Those things are not what have made Alice sick; they are trying to make her better. Still, Luke can't bear to look at them.

'That's a lovely thought,' Mrs Beech says. 'We brought Alice's iPod in, hoping her favourite music would get through to her, but perhaps your playlist would be better? Different songs, different tracks; perhaps they could jolt her out of her sleep? Something has to, Luke. Something will . . .'

'Can I stay for a bit?' he asks. 'Talk to her?'

'Of course you can. I might pop down to the cafeteria and grab some breakfast; give you a few minutes on your own.' Laura Beech looks uncertain for a moment. 'The nurses are right here if anything happens; you just have to call . . .'

Luke smiles. 'If anything happens, I'll yell so loudly for the nurses that you'll hear me all the way from the cafeteria,' he promises.

30

Alice

'Hey; it's me, Luke. I promised I'd come back, right? Well, I made you a playlist; just some songs from way back, and some stuff I thought might make you smile. I think you'll like some of it, but if there's stuff you're not so keen on, just shout. I can always change it around. We could work on it together, maybe. Once you're better.'

I can hear his voice through the mist, and I jump up, brushing twigs and dirt from my dress. I walk towards the voice, slowly at first, then faster and faster. If I can just find the Hatter, I will be safe; I know I will.

'Why is a raven like a writing desk?' the voice asks, taunting, and I'm crying now, running blindly, stumbling around in the fog of my own mind. The faster I run and the harder I try, the further away the voice seems to get.

Sleepover

I'd spent years dreaming about my first kiss; the dreams had been based on teen books and American movies, shadowed with anxieties about clashing teeth and noses. As for the boy, he'd always seemed sketchy and vague; part rock-star-cool, part boy-next-door. It seemed astonishing to me now that I had never realized that the boy I wanted all along was Luke.

As for the kiss itself, there were no clashing teeth or noses. There were just Luke's lips, soft as velvet, his breath as light as a butterfly's wing, my heart hammering so hard it felt like the whole world could hear it; even I knew this was some kind of magic.

I didn't want it to stop, not ever. Luke's lips tasted of fruit punch and one hand burrowed through my hair while the other lay against my cheek, palm burning against my skin. I rested my head against the gnarled and creaking rope of the tyre swing and the two of us leaned into each other, perfectly balanced, swinging softly in the darkness.

Then Luke's top hat fell off on to the grass and we pulled apart, laughing, staring wide-eyed in the moonlight as if we'd never really seen each other before. Well, maybe we hadn't.

'Alice,' he said. 'This is not a party game, OK?'

'No,' I whispered. 'I know.'

'So . . . can we get out of here? Go for a walk? Talk? Please?'

I let myself step back, down from the tyre swing. Luke jumped down too, catching my hand, and it felt like we were connected in all kinds of other ways. Like each knew what the other was thinking, feeling, dreaming.

'We can't just leave,' I told Luke, though the idea was the best I'd ever heard in my life. 'It's Savvy's sleepover! She'd go mad!'

'We can do whatever we want to do,' he said. 'Come on, Alice. Take a risk!'

I wanted to go. I wanted to be that girl who would take a risk, do something daring, but I hesitated. What would Lainey and Yaz think? What if Savvy was cross and started rumours at school? What if Mum and Dad found out?

You don't just head off into the night with a boy you haven't seen in almost two years, not when you're supposed to be at a girly sleepover.

'I just . . . just wish we were somewhere else, that's all,' Luke whispered. 'Away from everybody. You know?'

I knew. I looked back at the house, wondering if I had the courage to run away, and then I heard footsteps coming along the path. Lainey loomed out of the darkness.

'Luke?' she called. 'Alice? Where are you? Oh! What are you doing? You were supposed to take seven minutes and you've been gone for twenty! We thought something was wrong!'

'Nothing's wrong,' I said. 'We were just . . . talking.'

Luke said nothing, but his hand held mine tightly. I saw a flicker of hurt flash across Lainey's face, and the faintest stirring of guilt unfurled inside me. I pushed it away. It was pretty clear that Lainey had a crush on Luke, and equally clear that he didn't feel the same.

He liked *me*.

My lips were still tingling from his touch; my cheek was warm from where his palm had pressed against my skin. Maybe Lainey felt hurt, but so what? I'd felt hurt, too, when she and Yaz had dropped me, cut me dead every day in the school corridors. I'd cried myself to sleep for weeks, until there were no more tears left to cry.

I refused to feel guilty for kissing Luke. I'd waited long enough for a little bit of happiness; Lainey couldn't begrudge me this.

'Looks like you two were getting on well,' she said, pulling our hands apart, coming between us, hooking one arm through mine and one through Luke's. 'But no time for slushy stuff now; Savvy wants to start her new game. You'll love it, and there's some hot chocolate on the go.'

Luke made a big deal of looking at his watch. 'OK. Look, I'm sorry, Lainey, I have to be getting back,' he said. 'I'm actually on an eleven o'clock curfew.'

'What?' Lainey pouted. 'You can't stay? C'mon, Luke, you have to. Savvy has loads planned!'

'Sorry,' he repeated. 'I can't get out of it.'

Lainey looked dismayed. 'Just a little while more?' she pleaded. 'I know where Savvy's dad's drinks cabinet is, and he doesn't keep much of an eye on things, so we could easily swipe a little bit of something to liven things up.'

'Nick his whisky?' Luke asked. 'I don't think so, Lainey.'

She stopped arguing then. I think she knew she'd lost.

When we got inside, Luke picked up his jacket and nudged the other boys and soon they were all on their feet, jostling noisily and saying long goodbyes. Savvy was disappointed, but she took it in her stride; she hugged each boy in turn, and when it came to Dex she kissed him on the lips and wrote her mobile number on his arm with black eyeliner.

You had to admire confidence like that.

Luke and I didn't kiss, and we didn't write on each other's arms either, but nothing could spoil the cloud of happiness I was floating on. Something amazing had happened, something life-changing. 'I'll text you,' he whispered. 'We'll get together; catch up properly, yeah? We'll do our late night escape another time.'

'Cool,' I said, but I didn't feel cool. I thought I might explode with happiness.

We trailed out on to the garden path as the boys made their exit; there was lots of laughter and hugging and flirting, and Luke leaned in close, his face in my hair.

'See you soon, Alice,' he said. 'I promise.'

31

Luke

When Alice's mum has gone, Luke sits in the chair, but it feels sad and wrong and awkward, so he gets up again and perches on the side of the bed.

'Alice?' he says. 'Can you hear me? I think you can. It's weird, because you're so still . . . so frozen. It's like you're miles and miles away, somewhere else completely; are you dreaming? Are you scared?'

He is hoping for some kind of reaction, but there is none.

'Look, Alice, I don't know what happened at the sleepover,' he says. 'I am pretty sure it was just an accident, but I wish I hadn't left you there. We should have run away, like I said. I mean, it was just a joke, really, because I wanted to be alone with you so we could talk. I hated all those fake party games, everyone trying way too hard to be cool and grown up – and I think you hated it too. I'm pretty certain of that.

'Lainey says you fell on the stairs in the middle of the night, that you had your coat and shoes on. I just can't help thinking that something went wrong to make you want to get out of there. I wish you could tell me. Everyone is so worried, Alice; the girls are really freaking out. Lainey is seriously not coping; she's ringing and texting me all day and all night, and it's kind of doing my head in.'

He sighs.

'I guess what I'm trying to say is that we miss you,' he says. 'Your friends miss you. I miss you. It feels like I've only just found you and now I've lost you all over again. If you're listening, Alice, I want you to come back soon. Please?'

Luke looks towards the corridor, in case the nurses are watching, but nobody is there at all. He leans over and kisses Alice's ear, traces a finger softly along the crescent-shaped scar that slices through her cheek. Her skin is cold to the touch, as if she is made of ice and snow instead of flesh and blood.

He picks up the iPod with his special playlist, his eyes blurred with tears.

'Alice, I don't know what to say exactly; I don't know how to get through to you, so I'm going to let the songs say it for me. I'm going to believe that you can hear this, and that you'll wake up soon, because . . . because you just have to, Alice. OK?'

32

Alice

'So here we go; this is the playlist I made for you. I've set it pretty low and I'll leave you to listen. I hope you like it. Can you hear it, Alice? Do you remember any of these?'

'Where is she? Where is she? Off with her head!'
Suddenly, the woods are filled with screaming, and playing-card soldiers are racing through the trees towards us. The Hatter takes my hand and we run into the fog, stumbling and slowing as the mist encloses us. Breathless, we hide behind a tree as the soldiers run past just metres away.
'I think you should go home,' the Hatter tells me, when the soldiers

are gone. 'The longer you stay here, the harder it will be to leave. And
things are getting dangerous for you.'

'But I don't know how to get home!' I say.

The Hatter takes my hands. 'You just have to remember, Alice,' he
says. 'You just have to remember, and you'll find your way back.'

But I can't remember anything at all.

Sleepover

After the boys left, the party mood crashed. Savvy was philosophical, already sending Snapchat messages on her mobile to Dex, but the others started bickering almost right away.

'It's only just past eleven,' Lainey complained. 'Who has a curfew that early on a Saturday night?'

'Lots of people,' Yaz pointed out. 'We're thirteen years old, Lainey. C'mon, admit it – we had fun. They weren't going to stay all night, were they?'

'It just felt kind of abrupt,' Lainey said. 'Did Luke say anything to you, Alice? Did you do something to annoy him? He seemed quite happy earlier, when he was with me . . .'

'I don't think Alice annoyed him,' Erin quipped. 'They looked pretty loved up to me!'

Lainey winced, her lower lip trembling, and I knew how much she must be hurting.

'We were just talking,' I lied. 'That's all. About old times.'

Lainey's eyes slid away from mine, her eyes cold.

'Is there any more of that teapot punch?' she demanded. 'This sleepover's gone flat – we need something to liven it up! We have the whole night ahead of us, and Savvy had that hide and seek game to play.'

Reluctantly, Savvy put her phone away. 'No more punch,' she said. 'And the hide and seek was going to be teams: girls versus boys.'

'We can still play,' Erin said with a shrug. 'We'll just do it the regular way. Who needs boys? We can have just as much fun without them, right?'

I liked Erin's declaration. Seeing Luke again and spending some time alone with him out by the tyre swing had been without a doubt the most exciting moment of my entire life. Apart from that magical twenty minutes, though, I couldn't help feeling that having the boys around had been massively stressful. We'd already been acting cool, showing off for Savvy; when the boys arrived, that had taken on a new edge. Flirting, competing with each other . . . the fun had ebbed away, replaced by stress, anxiety.

And when things didn't work out, we got moody, mean.

On balance, it had been a whole lot easier before the boys had turned up, when we were clearing up and dancing around the kitchen. Was I the only one to think that way?

'Sure we can; who needs boys?' Lainey said, a little half-heartedly. 'You set the rules, Savvy – is anything off-limits?'

Savvy shrugged. 'Not really. Just don't mess anything up, and don't touch anything if you go into my parents' room, or Carina's. And stay in the house, I suppose, or else the search could go on forever.'

'It could go on forever anyway,' Yaz pointed out. 'This house is huge! And spooky . . .'

'It's not spooky,' Savvy countered. 'There are no ghosts; or none that I know about, anyway!'

'All old houses have ghosts, though,' Erin said, watching my face to see if I was scared. 'The shadows of the past

'. . . of people who died here years ago . . . people who did bad things. Every house has a history.'

'I'm not scared,' I said.

Yaz gave me a sidelong look, remembering the times we'd spent Halloween together, terrifying ourselves with ghost stories and ghoulish pranks. Lainey and Yaz knew me too well; they knew I didn't like ghost stories, didn't like the dark. They knew all my weaknesses, just as I knew theirs.

'It won't be scary,' Savvy said. 'It'll be fun, and it might just burn off some of the sugar high from all those cupcakes! I'll be the catcher. Last one to be found gets to choose the DVD, OK?'

'OK!'

Savvy flopped down on the sofa, going back to her phone. 'Go on, then,' she said, scanning for messages. 'I'll count to a hundred. Scram!'

We ran. Yaz and Erin made for the stairs, but as I turned to follow them, Lainey grabbed my arm.

'Alice?' she said. 'Wait; I know a great place to hide. And Savvy's bound to look upstairs first, it's just so obvious . . .'

I shrugged out of her grip, undecided.

'Please?' she said. 'I need to talk to you. About us; about what happened . . . about being friends again. And about Luke.'

Her eyes were wide, helpless. This wasn't the girl who'd given me the silent treatment for a whole summer and then dumped me for Savvy Hunter; the cold, anxious girl who'd tormented me at Savvy's bidding had gone, vanished. Lainey was as vulnerable as the girl who used to sit up for hours at childhood sleepovers, telling me about her bullying stepdad, how unhappy she was at home. It was like the last two years hadn't happened. Lainey needed me, finally, and I was there for her, the way I always had been.

33

ICU, Ardenley General Hospital

Laura Beech is sitting in Alice's room in the ICU when there is a knock on the window; a quiet knock, tentative and uncertain. Looking up, she sees Savvy Hunter, the pretty blonde teenager who visited two days ago with her irritating mother.

It had been at Savvy's sleepover, in Savvy's home that the accident had happened, and Laura cannot help but feel a wave of anger at the sight of her. Alice is lying in a hospital bed, hanging on to her life by what seems a very slender thread; Savvy is untouched, unhurt, a picture of health and vitality.

Although when she looks more closely, Laura notices that

the teenager looks tired, her eyes shadowed and pink from crying, her painted nails chipped and bitten. She swallows down the anger and stands up to show Savvy in.

'How is Alice?' the girl asks. 'Has there been any change? Any improvement?'

'She's pretty much the same,' Laura says. 'She's off the ventilator, though; breathing by herself. That's got to be good.'

'I can't stop thinking about her,' Savvy says. 'I can't sleep, can't think. I just keep going over and over it all. I'm so, so sorry, Mrs Beech!'

Laura's heart melts, and instinctively she opens her arms as the girl steps into them. They hug, and Laura makes soothing noises as Savvy sobs and says over and over how guilty she feels, how awful.

'Savvy, it wasn't your fault,' Laura tells her. 'We all feel guilty, we all wish we could have stopped it happening, but the truth is, we couldn't. It was an accident, a horrible, horrible accident.'

She offers a wad of tissues to Savvy, who blots her tears, smudging her eyeliner as she does so.

'Another of Alice's friends was in earlier,' Laura says. 'Luke. It's great that you all care so much.'

195

Where were you all when she was well? Laura wants to ask. When she sat in her room alone, night after night, spinning out her maths homework to try and look busy, playing Monopoly and Cluedo with her little brother, drawing page after page of sad-eyed anime girls? Where were you all then?

She doesn't ask, though. She smiles and pulls up a chair for Savvy and asks if the girl would like a drink, and Savvy says she would. And then Laura walks away, heading for the cafeteria in search of mocha coffee with chocolate sprinkles; she leaves Savvy and Alice alone.

34

Alice

'It's – it's me, Savvy. I had to see you alone, Alice. I had to say sorry. This should never have happened. Oh, Alice, it's all my fault . . .'

The Hatter is nowhere to be seen, and the moment I step out from behind the tree I find myself face to face with the Queen of Hearts, flanked by two playing-card soldiers. She is beautiful but terrifying, cold anger flashing from her eyes. Her fingers grip my arm so tightly I am sure each finger must be leaving a bruise.

'Alice,' she says. 'Alice, I am disappointed in you. Why did you do it? Why did you have to spoil everything?'

'I don't know what you're talking about,' I whisper.

'Oh yes you do, Alice,' she says. 'You came along to my party and you committed a serious crime. You will have to be punished, you know!'

'I – I can't remember!' I protest. 'What did I do?'

'Why, you stole the tarts!' she says, her voice rising to a roar. 'Here she is, here she is! Off with her head!'

I pull away and the Queen grips me harder, and there's a tussle before I finally wrench free and stumble away into the mist.

The Hatter's words echo through my mind. 'You just have to remember, Alice,' he says. 'You just have to remember, and you'll find your way back . . .'

A memory surfaces, bright and sharp. It's the middle of the night and everything is pitch black, and I am arguing with Savvy Hunter. I can't remember why, or where, or how – but I remember falling, falling into darkness.

Sleepover

'What is this?' I asked Lainey as we stepped through the door into darkness. 'I don't . . .'

'Shhh, Alice; we're supposed to be hiding! Don't give the game away!'

The light snapped on and I saw that we were at the top of a flight of worn stone steps. The walls were bare stone too, and everything smelled slightly damp and musty. It was some kind of basement, and I did not want to go down there at all.

'Hang on, Lainey,' I whispered. 'I don't like this – let's find somewhere else!'

'I just want five minutes,' Lainey pleaded. 'Five minutes to talk, OK? Then we can give ourselves up; I don't care . . .'

I followed her down. At the bottom of the steps there was a tiny hallway; we pushed past a couple of ancient bicycles to get to three more doors: one room had been half-converted into some sort of utility area, another was being used as a wine cellar and the third was a kind of indoor garden shed. It was filled with tools and suitcases and rolled up rugs, an empty hamster cage, a shelf of empty jam jars and endless heaps of packing cases, boxes and crates. There was a kind of half window high up on one wall, with metal bars across it, probably to deter break-ins; a drapery of cobwebs hung across it like a sinister lace curtain, and if I looked up I could see the faint

silhouettes of plants and shrubbery. We were underground.

'Yuk,' I said. 'I don't think anyone has been down here
in ages. It's creepy!'

'It's just a cellar,' Lainey said, dismissive. 'Best hiding
place in the house!'

She dragged out an old tea chest for me to sit on and
perched on a battered garden chair herself.

'I bet Savvy forgets to count, anyway,' she said. 'She's
too busy messaging Dex. Seriously, she is boy-mad, totally.
Look; I just wanted to say, Alice . . . well, it's been so cool
hanging out with you tonight. I've really missed that. I'd
forgotten what fun you can be, and that you just, well,
understand me. Better than Savvy does, better than Erin,
maybe better than Yaz, even. We used to be so close, once,
didn't we? What happened, Alice?'

I opened my mouth to answer, but words failed me. What
happened? The Cold War happened, the slow dismantling
of a friendship. Bullying happened.

'I don't know,' I said, weary.

'I'd probably blame it on pre-teen hormones and silly
jealousies if I had to come up with a reason,' Lainey was

saying. 'And like I said the other day – well, things were pretty bad at home, with Mum's boyfriend. I hate Kevin and he hates me. He never misses a chance to put me down, make me feel like dirt. I was pretty miserable back then, Alice. I'm sorry if I took things out on you. I didn't mean it. I'd like to put things right.'

I blink. Of all the things that had happened so far tonight, this was the most unexpected and yet somehow the most amazing thing of all.

'Does . . . does that mean we're friends again?' I asked, hardly daring to hope. 'Proper friends?'

Lainey rolled her eyes. 'I've always been your friend, Alice,' she said. 'Just . . . well, we went off along different tracks for a while, right?'

'Right,' I echoed. 'And now we're kind of heading in the same direction again?'

'Kind of,' Lainey agreed. 'It's just a case of getting Savvy to accept you, that's all.'

'She's nice,' I said. 'Much funnier and cooler than I thought. Not so scary.'

Lainey laughed. 'Well, that's where you're wrong, Alice,' she told me. 'Savvy is sweet and kind and funny, sure, but

she likes to get her own way. She's in charge, and what she says goes. I think she likes you, Alice. She likes that you know boys like Luke and girls like Keisha Carroll. But, the thing is, Savvy doesn't let just anyone join her group.'

I frowned. 'What do you mean?'

There was a silence, and up above I could hear faint footsteps moving through the hallway, running up the stairs. It seemed that Savvy had finished her texting and started looking.

'Savvy needs to know she can trust you,' Lainey whispered. 'That you're loyal. That's why you're here, I guess; so she can suss you out, see whether you fit in. She's testing you.'

All evening I'd wondered about this, felt as if I was being watched to see how I'd handle certain things; a sleepover with the girls who'd been bullying me for months, a teacup full of rum punch, a game of spin the bottle. I had no clue how I was doing.

'You almost blew it, getting all mushy with Luke, y'know,' Lainey explained. 'The whole point of the party was so that Savvy could get together with Dex. The rest of us

aren't meant to get too serious with anyone. Savvy gets to say who goes out with who, so I'd cool things a bit there, if I were you.'

'I was only talking,' I argued. 'Luke's just a friend . . .'

I knew I wasn't kidding anyone, not even myself.

'I know you like him too,' I said, and I saw Lainey's eyes flash with anger.

'Ancient history,' she snapped. 'He's OK, but I have better things to do than get involved with some nobody from our old primary school. I prefer older boys, these days.'

I almost laughed at that, but Lainey had a way of turning things around when she was thwarted. If you had something she didn't have and she couldn't do anything about it, she'd pretend she never wanted it in the first place.

'Look,' Lainey said. 'If you want to be friends with Savvy just back off a little; stay away from Luke. I mean, you didn't know the rules, so she'll make allowances this time. But I said I'd have a word with you. Let you know how things work.'

My head was struggling to take all this in. What Lainey was telling me was crazy. I couldn't get involved with Luke in case Savvy disapproved? I had to prove my loyalty, let Savvy call the shots. It was messed up, and totally at odds with what I'd seen of Savvy this evening.

Then again, she didn't need to do her own dirty work; she had Erin, Yaz and Lainey to do it for her. Being friends with them all seemed like a lot of hard work if this evening was anything to go by.

Lainey jumped up suddenly, her eyes wide.

'Hey – what was that noise?' she said, her voice wobbling slightly. 'Did you hear it, Alice? It sounded . . . sort of electrical. Like a fizzing, buzzing sound!'

I shook my head. 'I didn't hear anything.'

Lainey was creeping towards the door. 'There's definitely something,' she insisted. 'How can you not hear it? Maybe there's a fuse box in the utility room, or a trip switch or something? I'm going to look!'

She slipped out of the door and I was on my feet, already halfway to following, when suddenly the lights went out. I froze, my heart thumping. It was pitch black; a stifling, smothering blanket of darkness.

'What happened?' I yelled. 'Lainey? Are you OK?'

'I think the lights have tripped,' her voice called out,

faintly. 'It's a power cut. I knew something was up – stay there, I'm going to fetch Savvy!'

Stay here? Like that was going to happen. I stumbled forward in the direction of the door, banged into something in the dark and skinned my shins. My eyes stung with tears as I edged my way round what seemed to be a pile of suit-cases with the metal clasps sticking out.

'Lainey?' I shouted. 'Hang on. Wait for me!'

There was no reply, just the quiet click of the door being closed at the top of the cellar stairs. My mouth was dry with panic. Lainey knew I didn't like the dark. She wouldn't leave me alone in a damp, musty cellar in a power cut, would she?

'Lainey?' I tried again. 'Lainey! Wait!'

I moved forward again, my arms outstretched to negoti-ate the piles of junk and rubbish. Instead of finding the door, I crashed into the old hamster cage and tripped, stum-bling forward against the shelving. I put my arms out to steady myself and a whole load of jam jars clattered down on top of me, smashing to pieces on the stone floor.

I stopped for a moment, heart banging, gathering my thoughts. I fought the impulse to cry or scream. All I had to do was stay still, and wait until Lainey came back with Savvy to fix the lights. But would she? Could she?

If something had gone wrong with the electrics, Savvy wasn't going to be able to fix it. She'd have to call an emergency electrician, and at almost one in the morning that wasn't really an option.

Moving more slowly now, I turned and began to pick my way across the cellar again, heading for where I thought the door was. I held my hands out in front of me and groped my way forward, fingers snagging on crates and boxes and layers of dust. After what seemed like forever, I reached the clammy stone wall and then, finally, the door.

Relief flooded through me. My fingers slid down over the flaking paint until they reached the door handle. I turned it, gently, firmly.

The door was locked.

35

ICU, Ardenley General Hospital

'I shouldn't have asked you to the sleepover,' Savvy says, hunched in the chair at Alice's bedside. 'I'd noticed you a few times at school – in art, in the cafeteria. I saw you with Keisha Carroll and I thought you were interesting. I thought it would be cool to get to know you, but it was a bad, bad idea. The others didn't want you along; Yaz and Lainey especially. They said it would be awkward, because the three of you had been friends at primary and then drifted apart; they said you weren't the kind of person I'd really get along with, that you were vain and annoying and full of yourself. They said you weren't worth the trouble, but

. . . well, I thought they were wrong. I didn't want to listen.

'That's a fault I have, Alice. I don't like being told what to do. I like to get my own way.'

She stops, shaking her head.

'And then Erin said I was just playing games, messing with people's lives, letting you think we could all be friends when really I had no intention of letting you into the group. You know Erin – she says what she thinks, even if it hurts. I don't think I'd have let anyone else say those things to me, but Erin knows me well. I suppose she was right, in a way, Alice. I make new friends and then I lose interest in them again. You saw the photo wall in my bedroom. I'm fickle. I like new people. I like making new friends. I am always looking for the person who really understands me, sees past the surface, gets the "real" me. Do you know what I mean?'

Savvy sighs and rolls her eyes.

'Oh, Alice, you can't tell me, even if you *do* understand. I don't even know if you can hear me at all. I feel kind of stupid, but . . . well, I have to say it. I need you to understand. I shouldn't have asked you to the sleepover because it bugged the others; Yaz and Lainey especially.

'What I'm trying to say is, I don't think they were good friends to you, Alice. Not really. I think they were a bit envious maybe – a bit jealous – and they really, really didn't want me bringing you into the group. I should have left it there, but I thought it might be fun to stir it up a bit, make them insecure. I didn't care if you ended up in the middle of it, or if my friends felt threatened. You see? I am not a very nice person, Alice. I'm really not.'

Savvy hangs her head, and when she looks up again, her lashes are starred with tears. She twists her fingers together, drops her voice to a whisper.

'Do you want to know the truth, Alice?' she asks. 'I thought you were interesting, sure, but that's not why I asked you along on Saturday. I was using you. That's the honest truth; that's why I wanted you at the sleepover.

'Remember I told you about that day I was out with Lainey and we bumped into Luke and Dex? I liked Dex from the start. I hinted that we should go out sometime; me and Lainey with Dex and Luke, but they didn't seem all that bothered. I couldn't pin them down. And then Luke started asking Lainey about you, Alice; whether you were still friends, whether you still did drama, whether you had a boyfriend. He was interested in you, really interested; and I was pretty sure that if I had a sleepover and asked you along, he'd come.'

Savvy sniffs and raises her chin.

'So that was the reason, Alice,' she says. 'I was using you to get Luke to bring his friends along, to get to the boy I fancied. And I knew all along it would upset Yaz and Lainey. I knew it would cause trouble and I should have stopped it, but I didn't. Erin was right – I was playing games, and it all went so, so wrong. I know you were angry with me, Alice, and you had every right to be . . .'

Savvy falls silent abruptly as Alice's mum comes back into the room with the requested takeaway mocha with chocolate sprinkles.

'Sorry I took so long,' she is saying. 'They didn't have mocha on the menu, but I pointed out that if they can do a latte and they can do a hot chocolate, then they can definitely do a mocha – and they did! Here you are; I hope it's OK.'

But Savvy is on her feet, wiping a hand across her eyes, grabbing her bag.

'Savvy? What's wrong? Where are you going?'

'I'm sorry . . . I just can't . . . it's too upsetting!' she blurts. 'I shouldn't be here!'

She pushes past Laura, her eyes streaming with tears.

36

Alice

'Alice, this is Mum; I'm just popping home for a couple of hours to see Nathan. Gran's coming in again to sit with you and I'll be back in at teatime with your dad, OK? Maybe you'll be awake by then; I hope so. Come back to us, Alice . . . please?'

The mist swirls around me like wisps of smoke, and I tread carefully, softly; afraid in case the Queen of Hearts or the playing-card soldiers reappear. Propped against one of the trees is a huge, heavy mirror with an ornate gold frame and, as I watch, the Hatter appears from behind it.

'Have you remembered yet?' he asks. 'Have you remembered how to get home?'

He smiles, takes off his hat and sweeps into a low bow, before turning and stepping right through the mirror.

'Hatter?' I call. 'Remembered what, Hatter? Come back, please!'

I push my hands against the mirror glass, but it's cold and hard and impenetrable, and the Hatter has vanished without trace.

Sleepover

My fists hammered harder and harder against the wooden door – so hard that my knuckles bled. I couldn't see the blood, but when I brought a hand up to my mouth to stifle the sobs, I tasted salt and iron.

'Lainey!' I yelled, so loudly I thought my lungs would burst. 'Lainey! Savvy! Erin! Yaz! Somebody help me, please!'

I shouted and yelled until my voice was hoarse, and then I sank to my knees on the clammy stone floor and sobbed. They wouldn't come; they wouldn't help. It was crazy to think that they might. They were the ones who had done this to me.

Stupid, stupid, stupid. Savvy had set a trap and I'd walked right into it, because I was too lonely and too desperate to notice it was there. Why on earth had I come to the sleepover at all?

I guess you can't get closer to rock bottom than cowering on your knees in a musty cellar, crying because you're scared of the dark and sick with shame because the people you thought could be your friends have turned out to be your worst enemies. Worse still was realizing that I should have known that all along. These were the people who'd been bullying me all year. Nothing had changed; they'd just stepped up the bullying a notch or two.

I had wanted to believe that Savvy liked me, that Lainey and Yaz could be my friends again. I'd wanted to believe that things could be different, that I didn't have to be a victim any more; instead I felt humiliated, tricked, traumatized. I was here to be teased, wound up and laughed at; I was part of the entertainment.

Was the power cut even real, or had Lainey fed me a pack of lies and then gone through to the utility room to flip the trip switches? I didn't know, but suddenly the whole concept of a game of hide and seek seemed sinister, pre-planned. Taking me to the cellar, locking me in – was Lainey carrying out more instructions from on high?

Shame at my own stupidity flooded through me, quickly followed by anger.

I'd almost convinced myself tonight that Savvy was beautiful and cool and misunderstood; but behind the smiling face and Bambi eyes, she was coldly cruel, calculating; the kind of girl who might pull the wings off a butterfly for fun. I was the butterfly, clearly.

I gritted my teeth and wiped away the tears, determined to find a way out of the cellar, not to let my tormentors win. Slowly I made my way across the cellar again, hauling myself up on to the cupboard counter that ran beneath the window. I stretched up to the grille that shielded the window, tugging at the metal bars, but they were solid and no matter how hard I shook and pulled them, they didn't budge at all.

Maybe if I could find something to poke through the bars and smash the glass, I could shout and yell until someone came to my rescue? I was groping around in the dark for something to use when the first few shreds of logic began to surface in my panicked mind.

My mobile, uselessly, was upstairs in my coat pocket; no help there.

I sat back on my heels. How long would they leave me locked in here? It wouldn't be forever; I wasn't in real danger. Logically, I knew that. Savvy and her crew may have been bullies, but they weren't idiots. This was a sleepover, not some elaborate murder plot; sooner or later someone would let me out, perhaps pretend it had all been an accident, a mistake, a muddle. Savvy would smooth things over, switch on the charm and turn it all round so that if I complained I'd just look like a wuss, a troublemaker or a victim.

I was probably all those things, but I didn't want to be, not any more. I was sick of being invisible, sick of slinking along in the shadows like a beaten dog, grateful for any scraps of attention. My shame was slowly turning to anger.

By morning, this ordeal would be over, and I'd be able to walk away with my head held high. In school I would ignore Savvy and the others, and I would tell the teachers the next time they began messing up my school books or hiding my shoes after PE lessons. I would speak out, stand up to them and fight back.

And if I had to do all that alone, then so what? I'd manage.

I felt calmer now, stronger. The panic had ebbed away and reason was returning.

That's when I heard the soft click of a door, the shuffle of feet on stone steps and the turn of a key in the lock.

I jumped down from the counter and picked my way across the cellar again, found the door and turned the handle. It opened, and I stumbled out into the little hallway, right into the old bicycles which were stacked against the wall.

'Lainey?' I called, untangling myself from the bicycles. 'Savvy?'

There was nothing but silence.

37

ICU, Ardenley General Hospital

The ICU is quiet when Lainey arrives trailing a metallic pink helium balloon with the words 'get well' printed on it. Alice is still the same, dark lashes fringed against paper-white cheeks, lips tinged faintly with mauve. She looks like Snow White after she has swallowed the poisoned apple, or Sleeping Beauty waiting for her prince.

Lainey cannot quite work out how someone can look so sick and yet so peaceful, so beautiful.

There is a plump, middle-aged woman sitting at Alice's bedside. Lainey knocks politely and hesitates in the doorway, and the woman beckons her in and explains that she is Alice's grandma, and that she is sitting with Alice for the afternoon while Mrs Beech has a break.

'Cool,' Lainey says. 'Do you remember me? It's Elaine. I used to be Alice's best friend; well, I still am, really. Do you remember, you used to take us to the park sometimes when we were little? We used to call in at the bakery on the way home and you'd buy us cream cakes.'

The older woman's eyes widen.

'Elaine!' she says. 'Oh, my! I wouldn't have recognized you! You look so grown up! I'm so glad you're here. Alice needs her friends more than ever right now!'

'That's what I thought,' Lainey agrees. 'I've been in a few times already. Well . . . once. I'd have been in more, but it's just so upsetting to see her like this.'

Alice's gran nods, and Lainey notices that she looks older, frailer than she once did. Is the strain of what's happened to Alice the reason her face looks so grey, so defeated?

'I was at the sleepover on Saturday when Alice fell,' Lainey confides. 'I was the first one to reach her. It was so scary; such a shock. I just . . . I wondered if I could talk to her alone? Is that allowed? You see, I haven't always been a very good friend to Alice the last couple of years, and I want to explain and say sorry – you know – just in case . . .'

Alice's gran squares her shoulders.

'In case nothing,' she says briskly. 'Alice is going to be all right; you know that, don't you? She is going to be fine; I know it in my bones. Trust me, Elaine!'

Lainey looks miserable, her lower lip trembling.

'Oh, I hope so. It's just . . . she looks so ill! It's scary!'

'Oh, pet, of course it's scary,' Alice's gran sighs. 'But our family are fighters, and I know Alice is fighting now to come back to us. She has her whole life ahead of her. School . . . career . . . friends . . . even that nice boy who came in earlier. She has so much to live for!'

'Boy?' Lainey echoes, her voice a whisper.

'Yes! Laura was so pleased – a lovely lad by all accounts; Alice has known him since primary. He was in that play at the school, I think. So you see, old friends do count for a lot, pet. And you have nothing to be sorry for; I know that Alice has always thought kindly of you, Elaine. She often talked about you. And you will have years ahead of you both to set things right, so please don't worry.'

Lainey turns away, her cheeks burning, her hands

trembling. She doesn't know whether she wants to hug Alice's gran or slap her; she just knows she cannot look her in the eye.

She wonders now why she came; the bright helium balloon seems too showy – too cheap – for this sad, sterile space. Still, she ties the string of the balloon to the end of the bed and fixes on a brittle smile.

'I'll leave you then, Elaine,' Alice's gran says gently. She pats Lainey's arm kindly and leaves the room.

38

Alice

'Hello, Alice. It's me, Lainey. I thought we should talk. I need you to listen; I need you to understand.'

I press my face against the mirror glass and take in a ragged breath. Tears blur my vision and roll slowly down my cheeks, smearing the glass. I can't get through. I can't get home, no matter how hard I try.

'You'll never do it, Alice,' the voice says. 'You've forgotten how . . .'

The Cheshire Cat is sitting in the branches of a tree just above me, all smiles. I'm so relieved to see it, although I can't help noticing that it has very long claws and surprisingly sharp teeth. I wouldn't like to get on the wrong side of it.

'I need to remember,' I say. 'I need to get home.'

The Cheshire Cat laughs. 'I think it might be better if you stay here,' it says. 'Life would be so much simpler, so much safer for you. You don't need to remember, Alice. No good will come of that . . .'

Sleepover

I was used to the dark by then, used to the hammering of my heart. I picked my way through the hallway and up the stone steps; I opened the door at the top. A part of me had hoped that the lights would be on in the rest of the house, but of course they weren't. My fingers slid across the wall, found the light switch and flicked it on and off, but nothing happened. Power cut. The world was still velvet-black, silent, but I didn't care because I wasn't underground and it didn't smell of damp and neglect and my fingers weren't snagged in cobwebs or grazed by broken glass.

There was no sound, no sign of the girls, but I was free, and all I wanted to do was to get out of there. I was fuelled by shame and anger, gutted that after all the effort I'd put into tonight, things had still ended this way. I may as well have had 'victim' scrawled across my forehead in Savvy's black eyeliner pencil.

Staying here was not an option, but as I reached the front door I remembered that my coat, holdall and sleeping bag were still upstairs in Savvy's room. I hesitated. It was a cold night, and it was a long walk home. I needed my coat; I wasn't willing to leave my bag either, and that meant facing my tormentors.

As I passed the ornate mirror on the hall table, I glimpsed a dark, shadowy figure moving through the gloom; small, bowed, but not defeated. I straightened my shoulders. My shoes clip-clopped on the tiled floor and then there was quiet as I crept up the carpeted staircase, clinging on to the bannister. There was no sign of the game of hide and seek, but then that had started almost an hour ago and I was pretty sure it had been an excuse to play a sick joke on me.

My heart was racing and my belly churned with a mixture of fear and anger as I climbed. As I got to the top floor, a chink of light appeared, spilling across the landing, and I could hear the low buzz of chat and laughter as I paused outside Savvy's door.

Peering through the partly open door, I could see Savvy

and her friends lounging about on sleeping bags and cushions, their faces lit by the light of half a dozen flickering candles – the posh kind that smelled of vanilla. They'd changed into pyjamas ready for bed, and they looked younger somehow; too innocent to be the kind of girls who bullied and tormented others.

I knew better.

'I'm just saying, it feels a bit mean,' Savvy was saying to the others. 'I know we said we'd give her a challenge, a test, but . . . well, switching the lights off and not trying to find her for a while would have been enough. There was no need to do the whole cellar thing as well – it's creepy in there. Horrible. And you should never have locked it. Yuk!'

'But I thought that was what you wanted?' Lainey asked. 'To scare her?'

'Well, yes, a bit,' Savvy said. 'I just think you took it too far, that's all.'

'You made *us* do a challenge,' Yaz reminded her. 'Or a dare, or whatever it was supposed to be. To see if we were the "right" friends for you. You made us go skinny-dipping in the lake in the park at night – don't you remember? That was worse. It was dangerous. We could have been drowned, or anything!'

'You didn't skinny dip, though,' Savvy pointed out. 'You kept your clothes on. And you only paddled, in the end. I let you off.'

'Still,' Yaz reasoned. 'You asked us. You said it wasn't a proper dare unless it was scary and difficult. You said we had to prove ourselves.'

'Did I say that?' Savvy sighed. 'Look, I was only eleven then. I'd probably been watching too many American teen movies. It was a stupid idea.'

'I unlocked the door again,' Lainey said. 'She's free. She can do whatever she wants now, OK? Look, don't get mad at me, Savvy. I was doing what I thought you wanted me to do.'

'You obviously don't know me as well as you thought, then,' Savvy snapped. 'I'm going to go down and see if she's all right; she must be freaked out. I like Alice. She's OK. Not at all the way you described her.'

'Oh, I get it,' Lainey fired back. 'Little Miss Perfect has you fooled too; don't you see, Savvy? She's a vain, self-centred little nobody. She'll get her claws into you and she'll get her claws into Luke, and she'll use the two of you to fool people into thinking she's cool, but actually she's just a stupid, attention-seeking little . . .'

I shoved the door open wide, unable to listen to any more of Lainey's spite. I think her words wounded me more than the whole being locked in the cellar thing; I had thought she was my friend, in spite of all the things she'd said and done. I'd never really believed that she would want to hurt me, but now I knew better.

'What am I, Lainey?' I asked, my voice shaking. 'You might as well tell me what you really think of me. Go ahead; you couldn't hurt me any more than you have already.'

The girls' faces looked pale and shocked in the candle-light, but there was a coldness about Lainey's expression. I wondered if it had been there all along; if I'd just been too blind to see it.

'You know what you are,' Lainey said spitefully. 'You know what you've done.'

'Lainey!' Savvy said. 'That's enough!'

I was too shocked, too hurt, to speak. There are no words for how you feel when you find out that your ex-best friend hates you, that you've been making excuses for her, blaming all the mean things she's done to you on somebody else. I must be a lousy judge of character, because Lainey had had me fooled. It was almost a relief to hear her say it out loud . . . at least I knew now what she thought of me.

When we were six years old, Lainey had told me that best friends were forever, and I'd believed her. More fool me.

Nausea curled in my gut; sharp and sour and dangerous. I felt unsteady, ill, but I tried my hardest to be brave. I walked into the bedroom, picking my way carefully among the candles. Yaz and Erin were sitting on my sleeping bag, so I ignored it and picked up my coat from the bed, shrugging it on. I lifted my bag, half empty now, and slung it over one shoulder.

The girls were on their feet, all talking at once, trying to stop me from leaving, but I shoved past them, furious. It was easier to be angry than to show them how much Lainey's words had hurt me.

'You can't just go,' Savvy argued. 'C'mon, Alice, calm down; it was a joke, a mistake, crossed wires.'

'I don't like your jokes,' I said shortly.

'OK, that was the wrong word,' Savvy conceded. 'We were going to switch the lights off in the middle of a hide and seek game, OK? It was meant to be a sort of test, to see if you kept your cool. Lainey got muddled and thought . . . well, I don't know what she thought, but you were never meant to be stuck in the cellar and nobody was supposed to lock anyone up. It was a misunderstanding.'

'Too right it was,' I snapped at Savvy, my eyes flashing with anger. 'I didn't like your test, Savvy, and I don't like your sleepover. For almost two years you've treated me like dirt, laughed at me, broken my stuff, hidden my books, trashed my school bag. That's bullying, even if you do get someone else to do your dirty work.'

'But . . . I didn't!' she exclaimed. 'I wouldn't! I don't know what you're talking about!'

'Oh, spare me,' I snapped. 'Everyone knows what you're like. I was stupid to trust you, stupid to think that asking me here was some kind of way of saying sorry. I must be the biggest idiot ever, because I honestly thought you might actually like me . . .'

'I do!' Savvy insisted. 'Don't go, Alice. We can work this out!'

229

I was too angry, too hurt, to stay. I shoved past Savvy and stomped down the stairs to the next landing; the others followed, arguing, pleading, telling me to wait.

'You haven't got your sleeping bag!' Erin told me. 'Seriously, Alice, you can't go now – it's the middle of the night! Stay. We'll talk this through in the morning and it won't seem anything like as bad, you'll see!'

'Please?' Yaz chimed in. 'Come on, Alice. OK, Lainey was out of order, but don't spoil a brilliant evening! Chill out!'

I actually laughed at that. I was to blame for killing the mood? Yeah, right.

Savvy tried to block my way.

'It's half one in the morning, Alice,' she told me, as if I didn't know. 'It's not a good idea to leave now. What are you going to do; call your parents? What will they think?'

I raised an eyebrow. For Savvy, it was all about what people might think. She was scared of what my parents might say, scared they'd call her parents and find out there'd been nobody here to look after us, that Carina had gone out clubbing and left us to run wild. She was scared of what they'd say when they found out about the cellar, the lights.

In the darkness, her face was pale, shadowed. I could just make out the remnants of her white rabbit nose and whiskers, and she was still wearing the fun-fur ears, drooping a little now. Behind her, Lainey's cat face smirked spitefully in the shadows and Yaz and Erin, though they'd wiped their face paint off, still wore their animal hats.

It all seemed surreal and faintly threatening.

'I'll walk, don't worry,' I said. 'I won't tell anyone.'

Savvy looked more anxious than ever. 'You can't walk!' she wailed. 'Not at this time of night! What if something happened? I'd never forgive myself!'

'So what? I'll never forgive you anyway. Not any of you.'

Savvy looked stricken, and she stepped back into the darkness, her arms wrapped around herself. I felt meanly glad that I had hurt her, even though it was just a fraction of what she'd put me through.

I tilted my chin and turned to go, and Yaz, Lainey and Erin stepped forward as if making a last ditch attempt to persuade me to stay. They were all talking at once.

'Think of it this way, Alice; you passed the test . . .'

'Don't do this . . . come on!'

'Oh, for God's sake, stop being such a drama queen!'

That last one was Lainey, of course. She took my elbow and pulled me back, and I tried to shrug her off but she had hold of my coat. The two of us stumbled down two steps, and I put out a hand to steady myself.

'Get off me!' I yelled.

It happened so quickly. Lainey's hand dug so hard into my arm that I winced in pain, and her breath was hot in my ear. 'Go home, Alice,' she whispered. 'Get out of here and don't come back. I don't care if you get murdered walking home; I don't care if you walk under a car – I don't care about you *at all*. I hate you, Alice Beech. I hate you and I don't want you here. Stay away from me and stay away from Savvy and stay away from Luke Miller!'

I jerked away from her, but as I twisted out of her grip I stumbled in the dark, dropped my bag and tripped. Suddenly I was falling, falling, falling into the darkness.

39

ICU, Ardenley General Hospital

'I'm sorry, Alice,' Lainey says. 'I'm really sorry it had to turn out this way. We used to be friends; best friends, do you remember? We did everything together. We shared secrets, hopes, dreams . . . all that stuff. Remember?'

She sits down on the edge of the bed, smiling.

'Then we grew up, and I suppose we grew apart; the magazines say it happens a lot, right? I feel a bit mean saying it, Alice, but – well, you started to get on my nerves. You were so full of yourself; too keen, too chirpy. You tried too hard . . . Miss Goody Two-Shoes. I'm only saying what I thought back then, Alice. No offence. You got too big for your boots . . . all that drama stuff went to your head.'

Lainey sighs, smoothing down the bedcover, straightening the sheet.

'All that chat about Luke. Every day, over and over; Luke said this, Luke said that . . . like he was some kind of dream boy. You knew I liked Luke, Alice. I'd liked him for years; it was one of those secrets we shared. We promised we'd never let a boy come between us, but your promise didn't mean a thing, did it, Alice? You barely noticed he was alive for most of primary school, and then, the minute you were in that stupid play together, that was that. You forgot your promises; you forgot me.'

Lainey laughs. 'It's not that I bear a grudge,' she says. 'I just find it hard to forgive, sometimes, you know? Besides, you were a bit of a pathetic friend. I can't say I missed you when we stopped hanging out; Yaz was always more fun and Savvy and Erin were awesome. I was happy. And then you messed it up all over again . . .'

Lainey edges a little closer, her voice cold.

'When we met Luke and Dex by accident I knew that was my chance to make Luke notice me. We talked and talked, but all he wanted to know about was you. What were you doing; why didn't you do drama any more; did you have a boyfriend. It made me sick, Alice. Seriously. And then Savvy had her bright idea of asking you to the sleepover and this whole stupid nightmare began.

'You can't help it, can you? You just have to take the things I want away from me. The lead role in the school play, the boy I've been crushing on since I was nine years old, even Savvy. Did I tell you she's gone into some kind of meltdown about all this? She's all eaten up with guilt and fear, not like herself at all, and that's your fault, Alice Beech. You wanted everything I had, didn't you? It's just the way you work. Do you want to know the truth? I'm not sorry I shut you in the cellar. You made me so mad, so angry. You're so stupid you couldn't even tell when you weren't wanted; you couldn't go quietly. You had to make a fuss and argue, and you had to go and fall. You ruined everything for everybody, and yet you're the one getting all the sympathy. So typical!'

Lainey bites her lip and takes in a ragged breath. Her eyes well with tears that spill over and roll down her cheeks relentlessly, and when she speaks again, her voice is shaking.

'He came to see you again, didn't he?' she asks. 'Luke, I mean. Your gran said. He's not going to hang around and

wait for you forever, you know. Nobody would expect him to do that.

'I don't even think you can hear me, can you? What's the point of telling you any of this? You're just hanging on, being kept alive by the doctors and these stupid machines. Your family might be kidding themselves you'll get better, but I think they're wrong. I don't think you'd want to be like this, Alice – useless, out of it, like . . . like some kind of vegetable. It's just cruel, wrong.'

Lainey wipes her eyes, tries to smile.

'I don't even know what these things are doing: all these wires, all this buzzing and bleeping. Doesn't it get on your nerves? Doesn't it bug you? It would me. Sometimes the best, kindest thing to do is to just let go. I'm telling you this as a friend, Alice, for old times' sake . . .'

Lainey's fingers reach out towards the wires connecting the nearest monitor to Alice's chest, as if she might grab them and tear them away; but her hands are trembling so much she cannot make the connection and abruptly she steps back, sobbing harder, as if shocked at what she has almost done.

'I wouldn't, Alice,' she gasps. 'You know that, right? I

can't bear seeing you like this, but I wouldn't hurt you. I didn't mean you to fall; it's just that I was angry and you were too, and it was dark. Is it too late, Alice? Do you ever wish you could just go back and do things differently?'

Without warning, the nearest monitor begins to emit a high-pitched shrieking sound, and the electronic trace flat-lines.

Lainey screams.

40

Alice

'Help!' Lainey screeches, her voice rising above the shriek of the monitor. 'Help, somebody! Quick!'

When the memories come back, they come back in such a flood that I think my head will explode, my heart break.

'You have to remember if you want to find your way back,' the Hatter had said, but he didn't tell me that remembering would bring such pain. Every bit of me hurts, and above me – high up in the tree – the Cheshire Cat is laughing. It's a cruel kind of laugh; I know that now.

'Be careful, Alice,' it taunts. 'You might not like what you find on the other side . . .'

Even so, I need to get home.

I push against the looking glass again and this time the surface is soft beneath my palm, like gauze. At my touch, the glass melts into a kind of silvery mist and I take a deep breath and push through.

It's chaos. I am in a small white room, brightly lit and filled with machines that bleep and buzz and screech. I don't know why I am here or what is happening or why Lainey is there, why she is screaming. My body is roaring, railing, raw with pain, and then suddenly the pain drops away completely and I feel myself slide effortlessly free.

I am lighter than air, floating high above the madness, invisible.

I watch as Lainey runs into the hallway, yelling hysterically, as two nurses and a doctor run into the room and gather round the broken girl on the bed. It takes me a moment to understand that the girl is me; she seems so small, so pale, so lifeless. I feel curiously detached as I watch the medics work on her, yelling instructions and moving swiftly and expertly to stabilize her.

'Come on,' the doctor says. 'Stay with me, Alice!'

I've been lost in a dark, surreal world of dreams and half-formed memories, and I think I stayed too long in Wonderland; I stepped *through the looking glass, but I can't come back, no matter what. There is nothing to come back to. The girl I used to be is broken beyond repair.*

I move between the medics, trail a finger along the cheek of the girl in the bed. Six days ago I looked at the world through her blue eyes, felt my heart flutter and race with excitement, my cheeks blush darkly when the coolest boy I knew looked my way. Six days ago my lips learned what it was like to be kissed and my hands found out what it was like to be wrapped tightly around the hands of another.

Will I leave all that behind me now? I know it ought to matter, but it feels trivial, unimportant somehow. It's not enough to make me stay.

'Please be all right, please be all right, please be all right,' Lainey repeats, outside in the corridor now, her face pressed against the cold glass of the viewing window. I drift out to join her and lean against her, reach up a hand to wipe away her tears, but she shivers violently and pulls away.

'Lainey?' I whisper, and her eyes open wide with terror. For a moment, I think she can see me, but she shakes her head and looks right through me as though I'm not here at all.

Maybe I'm not.

In the distance I see my grandmother walking along the corridor,

240

returning from the family room with a cup of tea and her knitting bag. She seems older than I remember; she limps a little and her shoulders are hunched as if she's carrying something sad, something heavy.

How will she look when she sees what's happening? Will I have to watch her talking to Mum and Dad and Nathan, see them all hanging on to each other, trying to make sense of it all? That doesn't seem right. Will I be able to stay for long enough to watch my own funeral, see my family dressed in black, see which pupils and teachers from school turn up? Will Savvy? Will Lainey? Will Luke?

And what happens then?

I can't even begin to think about that.

Out of nowhere, a hand closes over mine; Lainey's.

'I'm sorry, Alice,' she says. 'Please don't go . . .'

Abruptly there is a commotion inside the room; one of the nurses puts a hand over her mouth, tilts her head back and laughs with relief. The machines and monitors begin to bleep and buzz again, their neat electronic patterns resuming a regular pattern.

I'm not with Lainey any more; I can't see Gran or watch what's happening in the little hospital room, because I am back in my body and all of this is happening to me.

'We have a heartbeat,' the doctor is saying. 'Strong and steady. But something's going on, I think . . .'

'She's responding,' one of the nurses says. 'I'm almost sure . . .'

And then I open my eyes for the first time in six days.

41

Falling

When I look back at it all, I remember everything in slow motion.

I fell head over heels, tumbling, my body tucked into a ball, my knees and elbows and curving back, scraping and thumping against each step. It was dark, and that feeling of falling was more terrifying than anything I'd ever known in my life, so when the scream filled my ears I thought it must be me.

It wasn't, though; I think it was probably Savvy.

I bumped and crashed my way to the bottom of the stairs, and at the bottom I fell against the hall table and brought the antique mirror crashing down on me. Everything fell, everything smashed – even the glass vase of red and white roses that was on the hall table. Water and roses and broken glass and shards of mirror were scattered everywhere.

My head hit the tiled floor and everything vanished – including me.

42

Fallen

My last memory from the night of the fall was looking down on myself as I lay crumpled and unconscious in the hallway, after Savvy had run down to the cellar to switch the lights back on. The girls had sobbed and argued and finally lifted the big antique mirror off me, leaning what was left of it against the far wall. It was ruined – exploded – as if I had dived through its glassy surface mistaking it for water; the evidence of the splash was everywhere. I had dived right through its surface to the other side, and I was lost.

Once they had moved the mirror, the girls gathered round me; shocked, tearful, debating what to do and who should call the emergency services, but I was above it all, impassive, looking down.

I looked like a broken doll. My arms and legs were flung out at slightly improbable angles and my hair was spread out around my head like a crimped, golden brown halo. My eyes were closed as if I were sleeping, but the left side of my face was covered in blood where the broken vase had sliced into my cheek. My skirt had rucked up a little, showing layers of lace and net petticoats, and the red and white roses had fallen across my body like funeral flowers.

Everywhere, glinting like diamonds in the light, were jagged shards of mirror glass. Some were tiny, sprinkled across my dress like a scattering of stars. It looked like someone had sewn them on to the blue, but if you looked carefully you could see the same tiny mirror glass diamonds like dust on my skin, in my hair, on the tiled floor all around me. Some of the shards were huge, like daggers, and these were everywhere too.

Don't touch, the glass shards warned. Don't touch, or I will hurt you the way you've hurt me.

43

Alice

I open my eyes to see doctors and nurses crowding in on me; to smiles, laughter, relief. Then Gran is there, her arms around me, and I drift back to life within her warm, soft, talcum-powder embrace. I see Lainey lurking uncertainly in the doorway and I want to thank her for taking my hand and asking me to stay, but my tongue is as dry as sawdust and as stiff as old shoe leather in my parched throat, and she slips away quietly before I can say anything at all.

Then Mum and Dad are here, and Nate; he curls up beside me on the coverlet, holding my hand, and even though this is against the rules the nurses don't say a thing.

I am still ill and exhausted, sleeping a lot and crying a lot, too. Once when I wake up briefly, Luke is there; in my half-asleep state I mistake him for the Hatter, his wavy hair unruly, his grin bright enough to light up the dark.

He ducks down to drop a kiss at the corner of my mouth, and it feels softer than butterfly wings.

'You made it back, then,' he grins.

I stay in the hospital for another three weeks. Recovering from a head injury takes time; there are scans and tests for everything under the sun, but it seems there is no lasting damage. The doctors conclude that my body created a state of coma to protect it from the pain of my injuries; a prolonged period of rest and healing. The doctors have no logical explanation though for why the machines went haywire and my heart stopped, other than to say that the body sometimes reacts in strange and unexpected ways. I am left to draw my own conclusions.

I don't try to work it out in scientific terms. I think maybe I just fell down a rabbit hole into a different world; a place that was calmer and safer than the one I'd left. Being there was fine for a while, but finding my way out of there, finding myself again, wasn't quite so easy.

It took a while, because I didn't want to go back to the way things had been.

It hadn't been much of a life; it was miserable. I'd been the girl

nobody noticed; the girl nobody wanted. I'd been the girl whose shoes went missing after gym, who found raw eggs smashed inside her school-bag, whose homework jotter vanished and turned up in the playground bin. I'd been the girl who hid away in drama club so she didn't have to sit alone at lunchtimes. I'd been the girl who sat alone at home every night, every weekend, who pretended that she had friends at school and pretended not to notice the pity in her mum's eyes; the girl who'd cried herself to sleep.

I wanted more than that. I wanted a whole life; a vivid, techni-colour one, not the watered-down grey version I'd been living. And then I began to remember, and the shock of it jolted me out of that nowhere-world for good.

For a few split seconds I was floating, free; then I was back in my own body, opening my eyes, pulling in big lungfuls of air.

So yes, as Luke says, I've made it back.

I've made it back — but things are going to be different.

44

Now

Six months on, I sometimes forget about what happened, about the sleepover, the fall, the coma. It seems like it all happened to a different girl, and in a way I suppose it did.

'It's funny how things work out,' Savvy says, lounging across my bed, sipping her mocha and flicking carelessly through her science homework. 'Six months ago I didn't know you at all . . . and now we're best friends. Who'd have thought it?'

Who indeed?

Savvy and Luke visited me in hospital every day. It was Savvy who told me that the police and social work departments had been doing some follow-up work; a routine hospital blood test taken just after the accident had shown traces of alcohol. Mum and Dad hadn't registered this to start with, but once I was on the mend again they began to ask questions, and the whole sorry tale came out.

Savvy came clean about the homemade cocktails. She told the police and the social workers that Carina had been out all evening, that we'd played a series of dare games including one that involved blacking out the whole house and locking me in the cellar. She pretended it was her idea at first, but when Lainey was interviewed she told the truth, admitted she'd taken things too far and took the blame.

I'd told the police that we'd all tried the rum punch, but that it wasn't very strong and nobody got tipsy. I told them the dare games had just been light-hearted fun, that Lainey had been trying to stop me leaving when I tripped and fell. 'Why were you trying to leave the sleepover at one in the morning, if it was all just light-hearted fun?' one of the police officers asked. I told them I was homesick.

The police and social work departments closed the case not long afterwards; the law is hazy on whether groups of teenagers should be left at home alone, but it was clear that Mr and Mrs Hunter had had no idea there was a full-on party planned, let alone how it would all pan out. The drink, the dares, the accident – they were unfortunate, and there were lessons to be learned from it all, but it really wasn't a police matter.

Everyone stopped blaming everyone else; we let go of the past and moved on, and in a funny way the crisis seemed to have brought us together.

I didn't go back to school until after the summer holidays; it took that long for my injuries to heal, for the scar on my face to fade, my hair to grow back. By then, I was pretty close to Savvy. A friendship had grown between us: a real, honest friendship, the kind that could survive earthquakes, alien invasion, even turning up at school in the same pair of patent leather ballet flats. Although that would never happen, because once school started again Savvy called me every evening to talk about the day just gone and the one still ahead and to plan out our clothes, our homework, everything.

And Luke . . . well, he'd seen me at my worst, with hair shaved and chopped off in clumps, scars on my head and on my face, a broken arm, a broken heart; none of that seemed to matter. I learned to accept the crescent scar on my cheek, and Luke did too, pressing his mouth along the curve of it in a dozen tiny kisses.

'So,' Savvy says now, finishing her mocha. 'I was wondering . . . Did you hear about Lainey?'

'What about her?'

Savvy and I see a lot of Erin and Yaz, but Lainey has dropped right off the radar since my recovery.

'Is she OK?' I ask. 'I haven't seen her at school this term . . . is she OK?'

Savvy shakes her head, sad-eyed. 'No . . . she's been ill, apparently. Or maybe just ashamed to show her face; it's kind of sad.'

'Have you tried to call her?' I ask. 'Has Yaz?'

'We haven't really kept in touch lately,' Savvy shrugs. 'C'mon, Alice, she brought all this on herself. All those lies, all that manipulation. I think Lainey must be a very unhappy person, inside.'

'She is,' I agree. 'I think she always has been.'

And now it seems that Lainey has fallen down her own rabbit hole, into something that sounds an awful lot like depression.

The next day, I send her a postcard; a quirky-cool image of the Cheshire Cat sitting in a tree, with a scrawled message that I hoped she was doing OK.

There is no reply, and I wonder if she feels too guilty still, or if she is just lost in another world the way I had been after the fall. Like the Cheshire Cat, Lainey used to be all smiles; I never thought I'd see those smiles disappear, but they have.

In exchange, though, I've found mine.

45

Looking-Glass Girl

I stand in front of the looking glass in my bedroom, checking my reflection: the girl in the mirror is tall and slim, her light brown hair wavy, glossy and streaked with caramel highlights. It's shoulder length, now, but it's growing fast. Her blue eyes are bright and filled with laughter, and there's just the faintest smudge of eyeliner above her darkened lashes, flicking out into a perfect cat's-eye curve.

The girl in the mirror is cool and confident and beautiful; there's something special about her: a shine, a sparkle, something you can't quite put your finger on.

She's a whole lot different from the girl I used to be.

I smile. Yes, I wear make-up these days, but the school turns a blind eye because it helps to disguise the scar. They're very sympathetic about that, and besides, not long ago I landed the role of Macavity in the drama club's summer production of *Cats* and snagged myself a mention in the local newspaper. Their reporter picked me out especially: 'An astonishing performance from a teenage girl with talent to spare,' he wrote. 'Alice Beech is a name to watch.' My mum cut out the review and got it framed. She says it is the first of many, and I hope she is right.

I straighten my skirt and tighten my tie and grab my blazer and satchel. The doorbell rings; three short rings, as always.

'I'm off now, Mum,' I call. 'See you later! See you later, Nate!'

Both Mum and Nate hug me as I pass through the kitchen; as a family, we have learned that life is unpredictable, and that hugs help a lot. Even Dad has been known to ruffle my hair occasionally, in a gruff, no-nonsense kind of a way.

I open the door and Luke is on the doorstep, looking

cooler than any boy has a right to look in his Ardenley Academy uniform. He slides an arm around my waist and we walk to school together, the way we do every morning. Sometimes we talk about drama club and run through lines with each other, sometimes we talk about friends, sometimes about school and homework and family stuff. We never run out of words, except when actions are needed. When we get to the school gates, we loiter for a while under the branches of the big sycamore tree. We hold hands and smile a lot and, if it's quiet, we kiss. We have had a lot of practice with the kissing now, but I'm not sure anything will ever be better than that first time, on the tyre swing at Savvy's sleepover.

It's hard to get better than perfect.

Then Luke has to go; he has to catch a bus across town to the Academy. 'See you tonight?' he calls over his shoulder, and I laugh and nod and watch him walk away, feeling like the luckiest girl alive.

When Luke turns the corner, heading for the bus stop, I go into school. I'm not invisible any more; teachers smile and say hello, kids stop to chat, everybody has a smile or a greeting. Savvy waits for me by the cafeteria and we buy a breakfast smoothie and head for registration, arm in arm. We sit together in every class, pair up in PE; I've even got her to join the lunchtime drama group at school, and even Yaz and Erin have been known to turn up occasionally to paint scenery or help with costumes.

Today, though, there is no drama group, and after morning classes the four of us sit in the cafeteria eating salad and chips and talking about boys. Savvy has finished with Dex and is seeing a boy called Mark; Yaz is flirting on a daily basis with a friend of her brother's, a boy called Ahmed; Erin says she is planning to join a nunnery or lead an all-woman team of scientific researchers through the Amazon rainforest. She says that boys are overrated, and her heart belongs to the Amazonian tree frog; the kind that swoops through the treetops in deepest Peru.

Across the room, Serena is sitting alone, eating a vegeburger and flicking through a maths textbook.

'She went to your old dance school, didn't she?' I ask Savvy. 'Serena. What was she like?'

'I don't really remember,' Savvy says. 'I think we were

sort-of friends, ages ago, for a little while, but I'm not sure why . . .'

I remember the photo of Serena and Savvy pinned up on Savvy's photo wall, and I smile.

'Oh – look!' Savvy says, grabbing my arm suddenly. 'In the lunch queue! It's Lainey – she's back!'

'She looks awful,' Yaz says. 'Well, no wonder!'

'She's really lost it,' Erin agrees.

I say nothing, but as I watch Lainey pay for her lunch, pick up her tray and wander across the cafeteria, I have to admit my friends are right. Lainey's hair is limp and dull, brown roots swamping what's left of the faded blonde dye, her skin pale, her school uniform slightly crumpled. She looks lost and sad; the way I used to be.

I watch as she puts her tray down next to Serena; I notice Serena roll her eyes and say something sharp, pick up her bag and leave. When you are somewhere near the bottom of the food chain at school, the last thing you need is to be seen hanging out with someone even lower down the pecking order.

I can't help feeling sorry for Lainey. She must be wondering how it all went wrong, how she lost her friends, her happiness; how guilt and regret poisoned things. She must be wondering how she ended up in the shadows, fading into invisibility.

The minute I started to get better, Savvy drew a line of loyalty in the dirt, and the others stepped over it without a backward glance; they were with me. Lainey was left to carry the blame.

Lainey hurt me in a million different ways over the years, but in the end she helped me, too. She went too far, and now she's nobody and I am the rising star of the drama group, Savvy Hunter's best friend, Luke Miller's girlfriend. It's funny how things turn out. I have a lot to thank her for, when you think about it.

Still, it's not nice being on the outside looking in.

It's not nice sitting alone at lunch, day after day, friendless, alone. I know, because I've been there.

I look at Lainey, her head bowed, her shoulders slumped, and my heart begins to thud. This is Lainey, the girl who'd squeezed my hand and told me I'd be awesome before the first performance of *Alice in Wonderland* back in Year Six; the girl who'd dried my tears in Year One the time I fell over in the playground and skinned my knees. I could list a hundred tiny kindnesses, acts of friendship over the years; had her jealousy and resentment wiped all those away?

I had no way of knowing.

Then again, Lainey had been the only one who could see me in the hospital corridor back in the spring when my heart stopped and the doctors were trying to save me. Lainey was the one who reached out and took my hand, who told me she was sorry and asked me not to go.

And now she is the broken one, the one who needs a helping hand.

The realization sends a shiver down my spine.

I have changed, these last few months. I have changed a lot; but still, I don't think I can turn my back on the girl who was once my best friend. Sometimes, you have to take a risk, offer a second chance – even to those who couldn't do the same for you.

I raise my hand in a wave, flash a quick smile in Lainey's direction and see her glance up, eyes hopeful.

'Hey!' I call over. 'Lainey! Come and eat with us!'

Lainey looks around, as if I might be talking to someone

else, as if there might be two girls called Lainey in the school cafeteria. She bites her lip and gets to her feet, gripping her tray of food a little too tightly, trying to smile. The attempt fails and she's left looking scared, wary, uncertain. She walks towards us, wearing her panic like a cheap Halloween mask, and I think how much things can change.

Savvy rolls her eyes and Yaz takes a deep breath in. Always ready to speak her mind, Erin is the first to comment.

'Are you crazy?' she hisses. 'After all that's happened, Alice? Really?'

But I know from experience that second chances can change lives, and right now Lainey needs a lifeline.

'Shhh,' I whisper, fixing on a smile as Lainey approaches. 'Chill. It's just lunch, right?' Savvy shakes her head, despairing, but there's the faintest trace of a smile on her lips. I think maybe she understands.

Lainey sits down and the five of us chat a little in a halting, awkward kind of a way.

It's not just lunch, not really; it's a kind of forgiveness.

A playlist for Alice

1/ 'Angels' – Robbie Williams

2/ 'Lucy in the Sky with Diamonds' – The Beatles

3/ 'All Tomorrow's Parties' – The Velvet Underground

4/ 'Alice (Underground)' – Avril Lavigne

5/ 'Girlfriend in a Coma'– The Smiths

6/ 'Tyre Swing' – Kimya Dawson

7/ 'Catch' – The Cure

8/ 'Bright Eyes' – Art Garfunkel

9/ 'Painting Flowers' – All Time Low

10/ 'What You Waiting For?' – Gwen Stefani

11/ 'Don't Come Around Here No More' – Tom Petty and the Heartbreakers

12/ 'Sometimes I Feel Like Alice' – Lisa Mitchell

13/ 'C'mon' – Panic! At the Disco

14/ 'Heads Will Roll' – Yeah Yeah Yeahs

Queen of Hearts Jam Tarts

Ingredients

- 12 tsp jam (any flavour you like!)
- 28g sugar
- 255g plain flour
- 140g hard unsalted butter
- 6 tbsp cold water

Method

1. Preheat the oven to gas mark 5.
2. Sieve the flour into a mixing bowl and rub in the butter until it resembles fine breadcrumbs.
3. Add the water tablespoon by tablespoon until it is a moist dough.
4. Grease a cupcake tray and cut the pastry into rounds larger than the rounds of your cupcake tray using a large cookie cutter.
5. Press pastry rounds gently into the tray rounds.
6. Spoon a little jam into the pastry rounds and bake at gas mark 5 for 12–15 minutes.

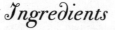